The Oldest Living Vampire On the Prowl

Rod Redux

This book is copyright 2011 by Rod Redux

This book is a work of fiction. Any similarities to persons living or dead is entirely coincidental

First Trade Paperback Edition
Published by Cobra E-books
Metropolis, IL

ISBN 13- 978-1461080862
ISBN 10- 146108086X

Also by Rod Redux

The Oldest Living Vampire Tells All
Menace of Club Mephistopheles
Mort
Hole: A Ghost Story

For Joshua

Liege, Belgium
12:30 am, December 23, 2010 A.D.

1

"Bitte! Bitte, lassen sie mich! Töte mich nicht!"

The man who just begged me to release him struggled against his bonds, making the legs of the chair he was secured to thump and screech across the floor. The chair was an antique, a French Louis the Fifteenth style armchair with a hand-carved frame. My captive's handsome, squarish face gleamed with sweat. His hair clung to his brow in wet tendrils. He was flush, terrified, enraged. The smell of his emotions was intoxicating. The rawness of it, the animal musk. The scent of sweat is almost as fine as the scent of blood to creatures like me.

I knew he was begging me to spare his life because I speak German fluently. I was born in Germany, after all. 30,000 years ago, give or take a thousand years.

That's right. You heard me correctly. I just claimed to be 30,000 years old. Those of you who've read the first volume of my memoirs already know this. For those who are just "tuning in", as the modern saying goes, please allow me to introduce myself.

I am the vampire Gon.

Rod Redux

Of all the vampires in the world, so far as I know, I am the oldest.

I guess that would make me the oldest living German, too. Funny. I never really thought of that before.

I sat quietly on the edge of my bed, my white hands clasped between my knees, and I watched the man writhe.

This killer, this villain: I had bound him to my sturdy wooden chair with duct tape.

Wonderful invention, duct tape. You can use it for just about anything. Fix a leaky sink. Patch a broken car window. Secure a man you are about to eat to a chair. I don't think the average person really stops to think about a vampire buying duct tape at a hardware store, but we do. I always keep a roll handy. You never know when you're going to have guests for dinner.

Maybe you think I'm cruel. Maybe you're feeling a bit of sympathy for my reluctant guest.

Well, don't!

He deserves his fate. He's a murderer, just like me. He showed his victim less mercy just an hour ago, when he killed her on the docks beside the icy Meuse, than I intend to show to him.

I hunger, you see.

The blood lust came upon me tonight with an urgency I could not ignore. I was sitting in my den, click-click-clicking away on the second volume of my memoirs when it struck.

I'd been ignoring my hunger for days as I labored over my writing. I am a slow and meticulous writer, if not a very talented one. There was no such thing as written language when I was born. My people sometimes drew pictures in the dirt, but even then, we had an irrational suspicion of such things. It was our custom to erase our markings after we made them, to rub them out lest they somehow influence our thoughts, or the thoughts of any who viewed them. It's not too different than your current superstitions about spilt salt or broken mirrors, so the written language, to me, can be a bit difficult, even after thirty thousand years.

As a writer, I tend to go back over what I have written again and again, obsessively changing a word here or a punctuation mark there, rearranging nouns and verbs because I subconsciously construct my sentences with a passive voice and it annoys me. She was going… He was doing… Instead of she went, he did.

I wonder what that says about me, this tendency to think and express myself passively? I certainly don't consider myself a passive creature. Being a bloodthirsty strigoi, I've always considered my personality downright aggressive, but maybe I deceive myself. Maybe my inability to end this long and desolate existence is the ultimate proof of my passivity.

So anyway, I was hunched over my laptop (see? I do it all the time!) when my stomach snapped down like a steel trap, making all kinds of uncouth, toad-like sounds. I winced at the sudden pain, baring my vampire fangs, surprised how quickly the thirst had come on. My stomach felt like it was trying to tie itself into a knot!

I should never be shocked by the hunger. The bloodlust is always there, at the core of my existence. It has been my singular and most constant companion all through the millennia. Sometimes it has the decency to mind its manners, and sometimes it's downright rude. Tonight, it threw an abrupt and impressive temper tantrum, stomping its feet and banging its head against the walls like an untrained child, stunning me with its urgency. The ferocity of my need surprised and frightened me.

Blood! I need blood now!

I realized I'd ignored my need for sustenance for a dangerous amount of time. I'd been rewriting a particularly vexing passage, unhappy with the flow of the words, and just kept pushing my deprivation out of my mind. I hadn't gone out in days. I hadn't even showered. I knew I needed to hunt before I lost all rational thought. If that happened, I would feed on the first innocent person who crossed my path. But first I had to get this paragraph *just right*…

When the blood hunger struck, bending me forward like I'd been punched in the gut, I realized there was no putting it off. I had to go now!

You see, I try to be a conscientious vampire. I'm not an evil or uncaring immortal. I try to monitor my blood hunger much the same way a diabetic human must monitor his blood sugar levels, because when I get too starved, I can be a real bastard! If I get hungry enough, I'll rip the head off a virgin nun and suck the blood from the squirting stump of her neck.

Being an ethical demon, that's something I try to avoid.

So I showered, wriggled into some nice clean clothes (tight, sexy leather pants and a black turtleneck with long sleeves; as a published vampire, I must keep up appearances, you know) and then I put my laptop to sleep and walked to my balcony.

Beyond the drapes and the frosted glass panes of my balcony door, the city beckoned.

Liege is a beautiful city. Say that word: "Liege". The sound of it is musical to my ears. The feel of the word on my tongue is a sensual one, but the city itself, the city is the real wonder. A million bright lights spread all around, and the traffic… traffic crowds the countless winding streets, even at this hour.

The Belgian city is famous for its vibrant night life. Even so late and cold, the boulevards are busy. Its denizens march along the icy pavement, bundled up for warmth, their breath blowing from their mouths in little puffs of white steam like cartoon word balloons. Christmas decorations blink and sparkle in all the shop windows. Cars honk. Engines rev and whine and burp. The sounds of modern life are so different from when I was born.

Standing on my balcony with the sharp December wind whipping through my hair, I suck in the wintery air and smile. I imagine I can feel the heartbeat of the city as it awaits me, eager, like a lover on satin bed sheets, powdered and hot with desire. The ebb and flow of its traffic is like the blood rushing through my veins, the living black blood we immortals call the Strix.

Anyone who saw me right then would have screamed in horror and ran for their lives. I looked like a real hobgoblin. When I go too long without feeding, my flesh turns chalk white and shrivels to my bones. You can see my withered veins, like squirmy blue worms, knit through the skin of my temples, my throat and the backs of my hands. But that is how a starving vampire looks. It's not a pretty sight.

Even when I'm not starved, it's evident I'm no longer human. My skin is white as marble. My fangs are long and sharp. My eyes gleam like fire frozen in amber, reflecting any light that falls into them. Peering out across the city, my city, eyes shining like gold lanterns, the sharp tips of my teeth curved out over my bottom lip like the canines of a wolf... only a fool wouldn't realize instantly what I was.

But I was all alone, standing on my balcony a dozen floors above the street, and I only paused for a moment to relish the chill December wind before I bent a little at the knees and launched myself into the open sky.

The high-rise buildings tilted in the heavens, swaying like the masts of a boat on a storm-tossed sea. Their glowing windows streaked past. I put out my arms with a beatific smile, my auburn hair streaming out behind me. Weightless. Flying... then I twisted in the air and landed in a crouch on the ledge of a neighboring balcony. I leapt. Clung to the concrete wall of an old office building like an insect (the strange texture of my flesh gives me this ability) and then I climbed. I scaled the building in a flash, dashed across the roof, and then I launched myself into the sky again.

I hunted: a killer looking to catch a killer.

And this is what the killer cat dragged to his killer home.

I hadn't learned his name yet. In fact, he'd just come to. The force of my accelerated movement, when I whistled out of the dark and snatched him from the ground, had knocked him unconscious.

I know firsthand what it's like to be snatched from the earth like that. I was a human once, and the monster who made me what I am now abducted me in the exact same manner. We vampires have prodigious strength and unbelievable speed. We can move faster than the human eye can see, and when one of us grab you at that speed, it feels like you've been hit by a bus. Or like the dark just made a giant fist and punched you with it.

I was sitting on the edge of my bed, regarding him hungrily, when he stirred and began the swim back to awareness.

First, he raised his head. He'd been sitting for a long time, slumped against the silver straps of the duct tape I'd wrapped around his chest. Body limp. Chin tucked down to chest. Breathing with a slushy flapping of his lips. After a time, he twitched his legs and raised his head. Mumbled something. He opened his eyes and blinked them-- once, twice-- still confused and groggy. As I continued to stare at him, mouth watering, he finally jerked completely awake and, with a curse, whipped his head back and forth, staring around my suite in alarm.

He noted my presence across the room from him and stammered in German for help.

I did not reply.

And that's how we remained for a time, me sitting there watching him twist and jerk in the expensive French chair I'd duct taped him to, my victim freshly awakened and furiously trying to free himself.

"*Wer bist du? Lass mich gehen!*" he demanded.

He was a beautiful man. I think that might be what kept me from draining him immediately. Like most vampires, I'm strongly attracted to physical beauty. It has stayed my hand in the past—as with my first vampire child Ilio, whose innocence stilled my desire when all I wanted was to feast on his blood.

Stocky, mid-thirties, with lush masculine features, my victim had large, deep-set gray eyes, a bulbous nose and prominent cheek bones. Not your modern definition of beauty. No. This was no emaciated mannequin, no androgynous whore with ribs standing out like the slats of a fence and sharp jutting hip bones. His was not the beauty of a starved and sexless skeleton. This was the beauty of the brute, the raw sexuality of the pillager, who comes in the night and knocks down your door and takes you against your will. The sweaty, grunting animal who rapes you in your fantasies. Who makes you come, even as he degrades you, even as he soils you with his lust. Generous mouth and square, cleft chin. His hair, thick and black and oily, shoulder-length and straight, with just a hint of feathered bangs. An expensive haircut and an expensive suit. Yes, he was a killer, a plunderer, a rapist, but a beautiful, wealthy, sexy monster, and looking at him there, I realized I wanted more than just his blood.

For simplicity's sake, I will translate all that was spoken between us from that moment on.

2

"You bastard!" he cursed. "Let me go, fucker!"

It excited me to see him struggle. I can't lie about that. I won't lie. When I set out to write my memoirs, I promised myself I wouldn't lie about anything. What good is setting your life to print if you are just going to make up a bunch of nonsense?

So, yes, it aroused me to see him struggle. It turned me on. If I was an actual living human, you might even be correct if you said it made me "horny". But I don't think in sexual terms much anymore. I can fuck like anyone else. It's a myth that vampires cannot fuck, but the blood… the blood is what satisfies my desires.

Looking at him, smelling the fear in his sweat, hearing the rage in his voice… it excited me. I imagined slipping close to him, lowering my face to the crook of his neck and sliding my lips back to expose my fangs. I pictured the terror in his eyes as my icy tongue trailed over the throbbing blue vein in his neck, the anticipation as I held back the ultimate moment as long as I could bear… and then…and then the splash of his hot blood in my mouth, the shocking force of its spurts as I bite into his flesh.

Ah, the image is so vivid! Hoarse cries of pain and revulsion. His fear makes me laugh as I sink my fingers into the muscles of his shoulders and savage him. I release all restraint. I indulge myself. Let the predator out of its cage. I'm in his lap, shaking my head back and forth in the crook of his neck like a wolf ripping the guts from a rabbit's belly, the meat in his neck splitting and tearing.

Bite him. Maul him. Chew his neck open. Blood gushing from the ragged wounds. Pulsing in my mouth. Splattering my chin and cheeks. Cascading down my cold, hard skin.

I lick the drying blood from my fingers when he's dead…

Shivering, I enjoyed my little pre-game fantasy. I rarely indulge myself like this. Normally, I eat on the go.

"What's your name?" I asked him.

He stopped struggling and gaped at me. "What?"

"I asked what your name is," I said.

"Lukas," he answered finally, his face still red and sweaty.

His fat lips curled as he spoke, as if it degraded him to answer me. He had the same look on his face when he took the skinny girl from the trunk of his expensive German car. I watched him break her neck and roll her dead body into the river with that same disdainful sneer. When I snatched him from the loading dock moments later, he'd smelled of sex and expensive sandalwood cologne.

His Volkswagen was probably still parked on the dock, its engine running. That's what attracted my attention as I leapt from rooftop to rooftop, searching for a soul to take, a black wicked soul to feed to the monster inside me: the sound of the car's engine, rumbling in what should have been, at that time of night, a deserted locale.

I was hunting the warehouse district in a rundown section of Liege. I often get lucky near the river. Bodies of water have always attracted predators, and I am the ultimate predator, one who hunts his own kind.

I zeroed in on the solitary vehicle, flying through the whirling snow to land at the edge of a condemned building. The rumble of the auto's engine drew me like the smell of fresh blood-- here to this silent, decaying plaza, where the streets were blocked with chain link fences and signs to warn off trespassers. He might as well have fired a flare into the sky. I crouched down and peered over the edge of the roof, spotting him immediately below. This man and his victim.

The exhaust of his car churned out thick clouds of condensed vapor as he knelt over the trembling girl. The white mist made the tableau strangely romantic, like a 1940's detective movie, one shot in black and white. Something starring the American actor Humphrey Bogart, perhaps. Or maybe a better description of the scene would have been "gothic".

Yes, they were like two lovers, clinging to one another on a foggy moor. The girl was naked save a pair of filthy, stretched out panties... and the zip-ties cinched around her wrists. She looked so used up and pathetic, her face a skull beneath her bruised white skin. A battered angel, fallen to earth, this weary girl-child, reclining weakly in his arms.

I didn't realize he intended to kill her until he gripped her head between his hands and wrenched it savagely to the side. I did nothing to stop him. I'd stumbled across the scene a moment too late.

One instant they were kneeling together like a flip-flopped pieta, the next there was a muffled crunch and an expanding pool of steaming urine swelling between the dying girl's thighs. I would have saved her. I promise. His cruelty took me by surprise.

I smiled—not showing him my fangs yet. For the moment, I kept them out of sight. "My name is Gaspar Valessi. Here in this modern world, anyway. I've had a great many others throughout the years."

Lukas regarded me as if I was a madman. Which I was. You cannot live as long as I have without going a little bit insane. "So? I don't care who the fuck you are! I don't care if you think you're Napoleon fucking Bonaparte! Let me out of this fucking chair!"

He ignored me then in a paroxysm of rage, jerking and thrashing against his bonds. He made the chair hop up and down an inch or two. The arms of the chair squeaked as he began to twist them loose.

I wondered if my neighbors in the suite below were home tonight, and what they must think was going on in my apartment. I've nodded to them in the elevator a few times. They were an older French couple, cultured and polite, he a retired banker, she his trophy wife gone *just a little* to seed. Not yet enough to surrender her face to the surgeon's knife, but soon I'd wager.

I live in an expensive penthouse and the walls are

soundproof, but I'm sure they could hear the chair thumping up and down on the floor, even if it was muffled. I wondered what fantasies the rhythmic thumping would inspire in their erudite imaginations.

I'd have to get his attention before he broke my fine antique chair and I was forced to finish this. I didn't want to finish it—not so quickly tonight. I felt like playing with my food.

"You like to say 'fuck' a lot," I observed.

"What?" He paused to ogle me.

"You like to say 'fuck' a lot. I think you like the word. Fuck. Fucking."

"Yeah, so?" He twisted at the torso. My Louis XV gave a squawking protest that made me wince.

"Did you fuck the little girl before you killed her tonight?"

He went very still. Every single muscle in his face and neck bunched up tight as springs, ready to fly apart. I saw his cheeks turn splotchy, and his eyes lost their focus.

Fascinated, I watched his eyes twitch: up, to the side, down. Tiny movements. Thinking fast. I could practically hear the gears in his brain whirling into sudden, frenzied motion, working quickly, trying to come up with some falsehood or excuse that might exonerate him. Finally, he squinted at me and spoke. "I don't know what the fuck you're talking about, you lunatic," he said.

I laughed, a little disappointed by his lack of creativity. So it was going to be simple denial? Unfortunate. I think he might die quicker than I originally estimated.

"No?" I asked.

"No!"

I leaned forward suddenly, my eyebrows rising, my smooth white brow furrowed. "You can confide in me," I whispered. "We're kindred spirits, you and I. I myself have killed. I've killed more men and women, more *children*, than you dare imagine. The things I've done in my life... they would make you faint if I told them to you. They would make your head spin. So there. You see? You can trust me to keep your secrets. You can tell me all the dark things you keep hidden in your heart. Consider me your confessor. I can absolve you of your sins. Wouldn't you like to tell me all the wicked things you've done?"

I cannot read minds, but I can sense the current of a man's thoughts, taste the flavor of them, by observing the subtle tensing and relaxation of the facial muscles. I can smell emotion in the chemical composition of glandular secretions.

The contractions of the pupils, the rhythm of the heart, the gleam of sweat on particular regions of the anatomy: they all inform. It is a skill that any human can develop if they wish. I've had 30,000 years of practice reading the body language of humans, so he might as well have written what he was thinking on a piece of paper and handed it to me.

Confusion. Fear. Anger. There was a certain degree of incredulity. He was thinking, *This can't be real. I must be dreaming.* There was also shame, and the paranoid suspicion that he'd been found out by an unknown enemy, had become the object of a revenge killing, rather than being turned over to the authorities.

Yes, I could glean that much from his gestures and scent. The way his eyes flicked from his bonds to my face, and from there to my clothing to check for a concealed weapon, and then the dilation of his pupils as he recalled the girl he had raped and then murdered. *Was she the child of an important man?* I saw him wonder. *Someone wealthy enough to hire an assassin?*

He was also becoming aware I was not what I appeared to be.

His gaze returned reluctantly to my eyes, stealing little peeks at my luminous irises before skittering frantically away, a nervous suitor, his conscious mind unwilling yet to contemplate the proposal of my otherworldliness.

He had noticed and was trying to ignore the chalky whiteness of my skin, and its odd, shimmering texture. More like marble than flesh.

"Will you let me go if I confess?" he asked finally. There was a whiff of surrender in his tone.

I tilted my head a little. "Do you really want to know the answer to that?" I asked him.

He thought long and hard about that. "You're going to kill me either way, aren't you?"

"Yes."

I smiled, showing him my fangs. I watched the blood drain from his face, smelled the metallic odor of fear in his sudden gush of perspiration.

"Wh- what are you?" he stammered, his gravelly voice going up a few octaves.

"I think you can guess the answer to that question."

"No," he protested.

"There are more things in heaven and earth, Lukas, than are dreamt of in your philosophy," I murmured with a smile.

He shook his head in denial. "That's ridiculous. This is some kind of prank. Did Maurice put you up to this? Is he watching from the closet? Maurice! God damn it! This isn't funny!"

"Your life will last only as long as our conversation," I said gently. "You will share some of your life with me, and then I will share some of my life with you. If you lie to me, about anything, I will know it. My senses are a thousand times more sensitive than your own. I will smell the lie in your sweat, see it in the quiver of your pupils, and then I will kill you, more slowly, and more painfully, than you could ever imagine. Now… Do we have a bargain?"

He nodded, his eyes beginning to glimmer.

Rod Redux

"*NO!*" I said furiously, jumping to my feet.

He quailed back from me, squeezing his eyes shut. I smelled urine as his cock gave vent to his terror. "No tears! I will not abide them!" I roared. "I will kill you right this instant, as slowly and as painfully as I've promised!"

My captive shrank back from my rage, his body quaking.

"You think you know pain?" I hissed. Coming close to him, our noses only inches apart. "You know nothing of pain. This pain you feel right now, this weeping for a life that is drawing to an end... it is but a fleeting sting compared to the eternal black despair I have suffered through the eons! I, who have buried nations of loved ones, a thousand generations of my own children... So don't! Insult! Me! Again!"

My teeth snapped shut as I bit off each word, just inches from his face. I could smell the terror boiling out of his pores-- a sour odor, astringent like bleach.

I sucked in his smell like I would suck in a mouthful of his blood, and the pleasure of it soothed my terrible wrath.

I had become a glutton for carnal pleasure over the course of the last few thousand years. It seemed to me that I had become not just a sucker of blood, but a sucker of all earthly experiences, the ultimate tick on the ear of the world, fat and ready to burst.

The smell of this killer's fear-sweat was as sweet and intoxicating to me as the smell of a virgin's unspoiled bloom.

I wasn't just hungry for his life blood. I was hungry for his Life.

I hovered near him as he trembled, grinning now, breathing in his smell, then I stepped away, a pleasant smile on my face, my sudden wrath forgotten. I circled my bedroom, touching my possessions idly, enjoying the feel of them beneath my fingertips. The slick surface of my cherry wood dresser. The cold brass of an antique alarm clock.

(I'd bought the clock in the 1920's in a little shop in Paris, and it still worked. Fabulous thing. Like me, it just keeps ticking.)

This is all I really have now, I thought. *My addiction to sensual pleasure, my earthly possessions. These things... and my memoirs.* I have not known love for many years. I was abandoned long ago by all my vampire children. Only Apollonius visits me now, and then only once or twice a decade.

Presently, I turned my attention back to the man strapped to my chair. He was still pale, shaking. "You know what I am," I said.

He stared at me with bulging eyes. He shook his head "no".

Violently.

I laughed. "Of course you do! Your media is rife with fiction of my kind. You humans slaver over every outré tale that is set on the table before you, so long as it invokes my race. Immortality has a sweet smell, does it not? But then again, so does rotten meat."

He shook his head again, then I understood. It wasn't that he didn't know, he was shaking his head no because he didn't want to believe it. His mind revolted at the idea.

"Don't deny what you know. It's insulting. I want you to say the word. We can't proceed without a common understanding."

"No," he stammered.

"Then I'll kill you now," I said, taking one step toward him.

"No! No!" he yelped. "I'll say it! Vampire! You're a vampire!"

"There," I sighed. "Was that so hard?"

He shook his head no again, but gentler.

"Liar," I laughed. I returned to my bed and sat on the edge, facing him. "Are you familiar with a book called the *Arabian Nights*?" I asked.

Rod Redux

He shrugged, dizzied a little by my sudden change of subject. "I... I've heard of it, but I've never read it."

I nodded, pleased that he had answered me, that he wasn't babbling hysterically. Humans generally react two different ways when they realize what I am: horror or hysterics. Very few remain rational after I reveal myself to them, and then I must take extra caution, for they are the most dangerous ones.

I continued: "The book, which is a very, very old one, concerns a Persian king named Shahryar, a man, we find out, who harbors some rather deep-seated issues when it comes to trust. Shahryar is a brutal ruler who, at the beginning of the tale, has been executing his virgin wives, freshly deflowered, the morning after their wedding. His first wife cuckolded him, you see, and so he decided that he would have his brides killed after their wedding night rather than give them an opportunity to shame him again. Not a very nice fellow. Kind of insecure, if you ask me. He probably had a very small penis. *Eh, bien... c'est la vie!*

"Eventually, his kingdom... well, it ran out of virgins, as will happen when you go through them like Kleenex. His vizier, whose job was to provide the virgins—sort of the royal pimp, if you will—finds himself facing the prospect of unemployment (probably in a very violent and permanent way, knowing the king) due to this dearth of unspoiled maidens, so the vizier's daughter volunteers to marry the king. You see, she's a clever young lady. She knows the value of a good tale, so she proceeds to entertain her new husband with a story every night, only each night she leaves off with a cliffhanger.

"Unwilling to have his wife killed until he finds out what happens next, he allows her to live yet one more day, and each night she leaves him with just the first half of the next tale.

"Well, eventually they have children and the king falls in love with her and decides not to have her executed, so the book has a happy ending, I suppose, if you put aside all the forced matrimony and murder, but I've always enjoyed the book, as decadent and amoral as it is. I've enjoyed it since the first time I read it in Ninth Century Syria, and I still read it every couple decades."

I leaned forward, my eyes gleaming. "I tell you this because I propose a similar arrangement. Henceforth, we will be Shahryar and Scheherazade. We will tell each other tales— true tales, however, from our lives. Not made up fables, as in the *Arabian Nights*. So long as I remain entertained, you live."

"And when you are no longer entertained?" my captive asked.

I let my lips split into a slow, wicked smile, showing him my fangs. "Perhaps it would be best for now to put aside such imaginings. I am offering you an opportunity. I am offering you a kind of immortality. You can share your life with me, and I will carry those memories until the end of time, or you can die with all your tales untold, and I will forget you like you've forgotten the dinner you had two weeks ago."

He looked away, his eyes narrowed.

"Quickly! Make your decision!" I prompted him.

"I would rather hear about you," he said slowly.

Oh, the devil!

He cut his eyes toward me, clever as a fox. "Are you really a vampire?" he asked. "I mean, a real one. Not just some faggot with teeth implants, dressed in leather pants."

"Do you not believe your senses? Have you seen any other man with eyes that gleam like mine, with fangs like a wolf and skin like marble flecked with quartz? Have you felt, from any other living creature, the cold that emanated from my body when I stood with my teeth pressed to your throat?"

"How old are you?" he whispered.

I leaned back, smiling. I did not bother to conceal my fangs. There was no need, and I must admit, it was a good feeling. It was refreshing to be my true self in the presence of another living soul, without camouflage or subterfuge. I so often have to hide my true nature from others. It is a kind of self-imposed exile. Even in a room full of people, the heart grows lonely.

"That's always the first question!" I laughed. "I am old," I answered him. "So old I cannot know my age for sure. I was ancient when your people first marked the lunar cycle on cave walls. Curious about that very thing myself, a hundred years ago or so, I researched the geological and archeological history your people have amassed in recent times, and from that research, I estimate my age at somewhere in the vicinity of thirty thousand years. Give or take a thousand years or so."

My captive, the murderer Lukas, scoffed at me.

"You don't believe me?" I asked. "Ah, well, it's a rather large pill to swallow, I suppose. Perhaps I can convince you of it during our exchange. By brunt of detail? No? Then I ask you to give me the benefit of the doubt. Suspend your disbelief for just an hour or two, and let me tell you a tale. When I am finished, then you can decide if I am an honest or deceitful creature."

Taking a deep breath, I launched myself into my story.

"I am the vampire Gon, and I was born a man, just like you, during a brief interglacial period in a fecund valley that was nestled among the mountain peaks of the Swabian Alb in Germany. I was born to a tribe of Paleolithic hunter-gatherers thirty thousand years ago, and it was from there, a happy fellow with many wives and children, that I was snatched away to darkness and made an immortal..."

3

There was nothing special about me, other than, perhaps, my uncommon height. I was not unusually clever, extraordinarily handsome or braver than my fellow tribesmen. I was a simple hunter like all the other men in my tribe. I had two wives, six children and a male companion named Brulde.

We called ourselves the River People, as my tribe never ventured far from the waterways which meandered through our valley home. We did not wander far and wide like the Mammoth Hunters who claimed the territories to the south. We had three regular camps, and settled back and forth, from one to the other, as the seasons turned.

My family and I lived in a cozy, dome-shaped tent, no different than any of the other families in our village. Brulde and I had fashioned our home when we were young men, after we moved from the shelter of my father, who raised the two of us. Our wetus was constructed of a curved wood frame that was bound with leather cords and had a roof of tanned animal hides. The tent had a couple flaps through which one could enter and leave and an opening at the top to let out the smoke of our cooking fire. Inside, the ground was piled with warm, thick furs. It was very comfortable. Later, after marrying, our wives hung decorations of shells and glinting stones from the ceiling, and our children played with figurines I carved for them from wood and antler.

I was very good at carving little animals and human figures, and I loved to watch my children play with them-- my beautiful little chubby babies. I remember how they galloped their toy deer across the ground, and how they made the little hunters I carved for them chase those deer, just like their father did when he went out to get meat for his family. My heart breaks to remember them now!

I wish I could go back in time and change the things I did that caused me to be stolen away from my wives and babies, but even for a creature like myself, time presses forward, relentless. There are no trails that double back.

Shall I tell you of my children? Do you even care?

Rod Redux

There were six of them when I was snatched away from life, when I was ripped too soon away from them. There was Gan, Hun and Breyya, and then our other three, Gavid, Den and Leth. I loved each of my children with a ferocity that makes my heart ache even now, thirty thousand years later. Breyya, my youngest girl, a little wicked snake, so quick-tempered and headstrong. My boys Gan and Hun and Gavid and Den, all of them bold and boisterous. Leth, our quiet little beauty, shy and gentle, always hiding behind her mother's legs. Of course, you don't love them as I do. No child is ever loved as they are loved by the ones who gave them life. I only want you to know how much it hurts to lose a child. Even thirty millennia is not enough to blunt the pain.

I only tell you this because I want you to understand what immortality really is. I want you to understand its unbearable cost. You think immortality a wondrous thing? Come back and tell me you still believe that when you have lost every single person you have ever loved.

Time steals them away from you, all of them, like motes of dust in a windstorm. You grasp for them, try to hold on to them, but the wind is so strong, and it plucks them from your fists, and then they are gone forever, sucked whirling into the vortex, and all you are left with is your memories, your memories and your regrets.

A lucky vampire is one who lives but one human lifespan, who can still count the ones he's lost on just his fingers and toes. It's no tragedy when one such blood-drinker is destroyed, for he has escaped the awful torture of immortality.

For beings such as myself—a true immortal vampire—there is no respite from that agony. I see their faces when I sleep. I wake up reaching to stroke their cheeks, only to realize, with horror, how long they have been lost to me... how very far away.

Dust... Only dust...

The Oldest Living Vampire on the Prowl

You think vampires feed on blood?

No, we are whitened creatures that choke on bitter dust.

Better by far to live and love and die, than chew on dust for thirty thousand years!

And we lived! Oh, how we lived! Before the darkness came to our fertile little valley in the Alps, we lived so hot and fast. Our people were a peaceful and un-superstitious folk. We had no religion other than a basic reverence for our ancestors, whose spirits, we believed, watched over us from the heavens. The stars, we thought, were their campfires in the spirit realm overhead, but though we sometimes appealed to them for good luck in hunting, or invoked their names in our fertility rituals, we did not worship them directly. As such, we had no silly made up concepts like sin. Sin, for us, was foolishness, careless acts that endangered our tribe or our loved ones. And our women were our equals, not chattel, to be bred and imprisoned and beaten when they disobeyed.

We revered our ancestors, and we celebrated our sexuality as the wellspring of our people's continuation. We did not twist pleasure into shame to control one another through guilt and fear of ridicule. We did not make up ridiculous fables like our Neanderthal neighbors did to explain the motions of the moon and sun and the changing of the seasons. Things we did not understand were *Nunhe*, which meant, "who can know?" Blood sacrifice and genital mutilation were unheard of in our culture. We would have been shocked and horrified to even hear of such a thing.

Group families were a common thing in our society. They normally consisted of at least two men and two or three women, but were often larger, with as many children as the household could produce. It was easier to provide for a family in those savages days with a male partner at your side, and the burden of child-rearing was eased by the same token for our wives.

Rod Redux

Of course, disease and predation were common, so to ensure the continuation of our people, we needed to make as many babies as we could, so sexuality was very open in our society.

I think our sexual practices would probably scandalize you modern people, with your tyrannical, pleasure-hating desert god and your unnatural embarrassment of your genitals. I think you would be outraged by the things we did in those primitive times. Our tribe held ritual orgies. Bisexuality and group couplings were common. When a guest slept in your wetus, it was our practice to comfort him with one of our wives, or to comfort his wives ourselves if he brought them with him.

I suppose it was a necessary adaptation in an untamed natural world, one stalked by great sabre-toothed cats, five hundred kilogram cave bears and raptors with wingspans the length of two men standing. I remember fending off wolves in the winter months with my fellow tribesmen, and had a fear of the dark because one of my brothers was snatched in the night by a beast when I was a child. I remember his little hand reaching out to me as he was pulled into the darkness, how wide and frightened his eyes were, and I never let my children sleep near the edge of the tent because of that. I always kept them between me and the fire, as close to my arms as I could keep those wiggling little whelps!

Men and women were ancient by the time they were fifty, and the world ate our young like an insatiable beast, but we lived free of shame and inhibition. We lived in a way I don't think you modern humans can ever comprehend.

What of my lovers?

Brulde was my companion, my tent mate, my husband. He was a quiet, cautious man, steadfast and thoughtful. Perhaps you think it strange that I should call a man my husband, especially in these times when such a thought is so controversial, but I assure you, it was a common thing in ages past, a thing, even, to be desired: to have a loyal companion to hunt with, to fight at your side, especially one as brave and true as Brulde. Not a thing to be mocked or condemned.

A male partner was a good thing to have when there were six children and two wives at home to feed, when you had to shit in the wilderness, when you twisted your ankle far afield, or your wives were too tired to fuck.

And my wives... how I cherished them! My beloved female mates! In terms of beauty and kindness, Brulde and I were truly blessed, for our wives were both those things abundantly.

Eyya was our first wife, a dark-haired Neanderthal woman who hailed from a neighboring tribe. A gentle woman with an easy smile, that was my Eyya. Plump and smooth skinned, with wide curving hips. She was a woman made for ease, nights of slow lovemaking. How persistently we wooed her! It makes me chuckle to think of it.

Though the men of our village teased us for wedding a "Fat Hand", Eyya was a great prize to both of us. I can shut my eyes now and picture her large, dark, dreamy eyes, her sweet, full lips, how she braided her hair with shells and feathers and painted her skin with gold ochre until she gleamed in the sunlight, an ethereal creature, a golden goddess.

She was joined later by Nyala, who was fair like Brulde, with long curling blonde hair and freckled cheeks-- a little young to be married, our Nyala, and tempestuous in her youth, but she was good with the children and kept Brulde and I in line.

Nyala was quite different from Eyya. Thin and lanky in form, demanding and bossy in spirit, but a sly and resourceful female, a fine woman to have when it came to bartering for goods or spanking our brats for their foolishness. Her appetite for our cocks, when we curled in our furs for the night, seemed almost insatiable. She kept us informed of all our neighbors' comings and goings, too.

Sometimes I think she was the strongest of us all. Though I always favored Eyya for her gentleness and dark beauty, I loved Nyala no less for it.

Don't be jealous, Nyala. I've cried a million black tears for you-- not one tear less, I swear to you, than I've cried for any of the rest. My bossy beauty. My fiery love.

If there was indeed a Devil, I would sell my soul a thousand times over to have you lash me with your tongue once more. To see you stomp your foot at my forgetfulness, your hands on your hips. To feel your body glide, hot and tight, upon the spire that your beauty has erected in my loins.

We were a happy clan, the four of us, with all our fussing babies.

But then the shadow came, the Foul One, the terrible Blood Drinker who stole me away.

His shadow fell upon our valley like the night falls, fast and cold over the jagged mountains. He came as the seasons changed from autumn to winter, as the leaves turned orange and brown and drifted to the earth, dying at the verge of winter.

As my body was soon to die.

The monster who made me into this thing that I am... I never knew his name. His origin was a mystery to me, his age unknown. He made me this thing, this terrible undying white thing, and then I killed him.

I can tell you only what he looked like, and that, to me, a living man, he was hideous, a revolting ogre. Cold, white and powerful, with teeth sharpened in the manner of the man-eating tribes who lived in the cold wastes to the North, his body was gaunt and wizened, his eyes always wide, as if he only thought of terrible, violent things. He painted his face with black pigment so that it looked like a leering skull, and his irises gleamed in the dark like coals. A wild thing, a demon, he adorned his body in the bones of his victims, and when he leapt, a cloak of animal furs spread out from his shoulders, making him appear to be a great bird of prey.

He was not a true immortal like me, but to me, a living man, he was a god. A god of death. A god of depravity. A god of corruption and rot.

Thirty millennia is not enough time to cool the flames of my hatred for him.

My maker roosted in the mountains that overlooked our valley like some dread vulture and commenced to devour the people of our neighboring tribe, the Neanderthals from which my wife Eyya descended. When our hunters spotted the last of Eyya's people fleeing from their blighted mountain home, we sent a party to ask them why they were leaving, after sharing the valley and river with us in peace for so many generations. The fleeing Neanderthals warned us of the terrible demon who stole their people by night. Our valley, they said, had been cursed, and we would be wise to flee it as well.

Well, they were a superstitious bunch! we kidded ourselves. The Fat Hands believed the moon and the sun were gods who chased one another across the sky. They worshipped cave bears. They saw spirits in the shadows at the back of their cave. The world, to them, was a haunted place, full of ghosts and monsters and evil spirits. We were certain our neighbors were being hectored by raiders from some other tribe, perhaps the Foul Ones from the North, who liked to dress up in the bones of the men and women they ate. Those silly Neanderthals could spy a lump of mammoth dung and imagine in it a terrible demon.

Nevertheless, we sent a scouting party to their mountaintop home to investigate their claims. Eleven men set out that morning for the land of the Gray Stone People, which

Rod Redux

is what we called the Neanderthals. There was myself and Brulde, my father Gan and his older cousin Kort-lenthe. There was Tavet, who was a hulking bear of a man, half-Neanderthal like the young ones Eyya bore for me. There was young Strom, beardless still but strong and brave, and his tent mate Hyde, who sported a thick shock of kinky black hair and a big, bushy beard, unusually full for one so young. There came also the three young brothers: Halde, Tetch and Git... and bringing up the rear: fat, clumsy Bukhult. Of the eleven who ascended the mount, only two of us returned. Brulde, and my father's cousin Kort-lenthe.

My father was murdered by my savage maker, his head struck from his shoulders by the god-like being. The rest, except Bukhult, who died on the way, were hunted for sport the previous night. Kort-lenthe was the only one who escaped unscathed. My Brulde was nearly crippled, and I... I was taken captive.

My maker took me because I was the one who killed his foul pet.

There were two of them, you see, a master and a slave. When we approached the abandoned warren of the Gray Stone People, the little vampire attacked us first. He was small and fast, with the mannerisms of a lizard, and though he was the weaker of the two, he fell beneath my blade only after evading the simultaneous attacks of our four remaining warriors. He dodged bow and spear as he shot from the dark cave toward me, and in a fleeting moment of distraction, I plunged my knife into his heart.

I suppose my maker thought to press me into servitude, to enslave me as he had enslaved the little creature I'd destroyed. He was a powerful vampire, my maker, but not terribly clever. He was overconfident and cruel. He underestimated my stubbornness, and my desire to return to the family I so loved.

He threw me down into a charnel pit, a cavern full of dead

Neanderthals, and that is where he made me into this thing that I am.

Do you know what it's like to be made an immortal?

First, I suppose, I should tell you how it's done.

There is a thing inside every vampire, something black and insatiable. It is an entity that dwells in us all, a foul blight threaded through every vein, coiled in every organ. It is a living creature, but mindless. Formless, it knows only hunger. None of us know from whence it came, only that it is unlike any other living creature that crawls or flies or swims upon this earth. It is amorphous and foul, black as pitch. I have seen it come out of a Blood Drinker like a tide of horrid worms, and once watched in mute horror as it poured forth from the jaws of an ancient fiend and spread out in the air like the wings of a bat—which may be how that particular myth was founded.

Over the millennia, I have heard it called many things: the Demon, the Hungry Spirit, the Venom. Ancient Greek vampires called it the Strix. I refer to it most often as the Living Blood, or the Hunger. I've also heard it called the Striges, the Strigoi, and the Ebu Potashu, which means "black blood".

When we are hurt, it knits us back together again. When we go without feeding, it compels us to hunt. It transforms our flesh into gleaming white stone, enhances our mind, and quickens our senses. It amplifies our strength to the strength of a titan. It makes us into perfect predators, our speed inhuman, our pheromones irresistible. It preserves us. Protects us. Yet, ultimately, it enslaves.

When we go to make another of us, we put our lips over theirs and the Hungry Spirit comes up out of us, it comes up and a part of it goes into the other.

The taste as it slides down your throat is the foulest taste you can ever imagine. You feel it wriggle inside your mouth, squirm its way down your throat. You feel it wiggle down into your guts, and then the pain and the cold threads out through your limbs. You feel it moving through your arms. Worming its way down your legs. You thrash and scream as it knits itself through your entire being.

It pierces your heart. It sinks hooks in your brain. Pain! So much pain! You pray for death as its grip on you tightens. Make it stop! Oh, please, make it stop! And then, when it has filled you, when it has joined with every mote and molecule in your body, you feel the coldness spreading, and you hold your hand up before your eyes and see your warm, soft flesh begin to blanch. You see your flesh turn to stone, your nails turn to glass. The bones of your face suddenly crack and pop as your eyeteeth elongate into wolf-like fangs. The light stings your eyes, flashing like a bolt of lightning, as the transformation moves upwards into your skull. You feel your brain throb, and your thoughts begin to fly. Faster. Faster. You see… everything. You smell… everything. Every inch of the surface of your body becomes a thrumming organ of sensation. No! It's too much! And then…

And then the darkness. Your brain overloaded, you slump into unconsciousness. A stupor, like death. You lie there, inert, as the Strix finishes its work. As it perfects you. As it removes you from time.

You awaken transformed.

A demon. A fiend.

You awaken, a predator.

When my maker descended into the charnel pit to make me his slave, he wrestled me to the ground, pried open my mouth, and vomited the Living Blood into my maw. He thought to make me his slave, but there was one thing he didn't know. He didn't know that, sometimes, very rarely, the black blood creates a whitened god.

I was remade into a being of enormous power. A true immortal. Drive a blade through my heart and I pluck it out like a thorn. Cut off my head, and I will bend to place it back on my neck. I have tried countless methods to destroy this body throughout the millennia, and each time I have failed. My flesh doesn't burn. Corrosives drip right off me. I have thrown myself from great heights, shattering at the bottom like china, only to find the slivers drawn back together. I cannot drown. I do not become sick. I am an immortal, and my master, who was an imperfect Blood Drinker, met his fate at my hands.

I thought to return to my family when I was free, but my blood-thirst was new and fresh and ravening. The first member of my tribe who crossed my path died to slake my thirst. Horrified, I stayed at a distance after that. I watched my people from afar. I watched helplessly as Brulde and Eyya and Nyala aged, as my children grew up and took families of their own, and when they had all passed away, my children, my grandchildren, and their grandchildren's children, when the earth grew cold and the glaciers began once more to creep over the mountains into my valley home, I went to the ice to kill myself.

Loneliness had driven me insane. All I longed for was death. I flew to the glacier that was devouring my valley and stood upon the great shelf of ice. The wind blew through my hair as I stood there, looking out across the world, and I thought: I don't want this life anymore. This cold empty life. I am done with it. Everyone I have ever loved is dust. My tribe has abandoned this place. The cold is come over all, and I am finished. And thinking that, I found a deep and jagged crevasse in the creeping white leviathan and I threw myself inside.

I thought, *Surely this will end me, this crawling continent of ice.* And when the great shelves cracked and crushed me flat between them, and I saw my black blood burst out before my eyes, I thought: *Finally!*

But it was not the end of me.

Rod Redux

It was just the beginning.
I awakened, seven thousand years later.

Tundra
23,000 Years Ago
Earth Spirit Man

1

I did not know how long I'd drifted in the slow ice when I first awoke. There were no thoughts in that great tomb of white, no sense of time, no sense of self. I'd floated within the cold's embrace, insensate, as the glacier fileted the flesh from my bones and then ground those bones to slivers. For all intents and purposes, I was unmade, and it was a glorious release. Sweet oblivion. I can only imagine the damage it did to my body as the white juggernaut flowed, so slow and relentless, its snowy fingers clawing further and further south across the lands of Europe. I had no sense of myself, and if I had dreams, they did not follow me from the dark when I was reborn.

For seven thousand years, I slept in that womb of ice. I lay there, an insect trapped in white amber, as the world spun on, as the Earth chilled, as all the familiar flora and fauna I shared the world with when I was a living man shivered and passed away, and new orders of life flourished and filled the vacancies

Rod Redux

left behind by all those extinct creatures. When at last the Earth began to warm, and I was delivered like a baby into this new world, cast out by the retreating glacial floe like a half-formed fetus, I was, like a premature child, helpless and without memory, a new thing myself, and savage for that newness.

The first thing I remember is the smell of blood.

Of course.

I could not see. I could not feel. I could only smell, and I smelled blood.

My mind was like a dark and echoing cave, an empty gourd. Crushed flat a million times and repaired imperfectly by the living blood which animates my kind, my mind was a blank slate, a tabula rasa, upon which the demon within me scribbled its urgent and ghastly needs.

Must feed! Need blood!

Awaken! Awaken!

Eat!

Hot salty smell of blood, coppery and red... my mouth filled with saliva.

My mouth. I discovered my mouth then, and I creaked open my jaws and ran my tongue around my teeth, feeling the tips of my fangs with it—careful! They're sharp!—feeling my dry lips stretch and crack, like cold-stiffened leather. My jaw felt strange, misshapen, and there was pain when I yawned it open. I heard the bones pop and crunch.

Feeling my lips, then, I discovered my head. It felt oddly twisted and flattened. I tried to move it, but it seemed frozen, calcified. I pressed harder and felt a searing pain in my cheek. I heard a sound like small branches snapping. Why did it hurt so much to move my head? It felt like something was ripping the skin from my face.

I moaned softly, and in moaning, heard the sound of myself.

Sound. Ears!

I listened and found that I could hear a melancholy hooting, a thing I once called "wind". Carried on the wind was the resounding cry of a bird, wheeling high overhead, searching the ground for prey.

Screeee!

From the dark hole of my mind, a word swam up for that sound. *Lenthe*, or what you modern humans would call a "hawk" in your English language. I could hear the hiss of the wind in the grass, and the rustle of leaves, a dry ticking, as from the tips of brittle branches. Further away: the low murmur of human voices, the crackle of a campfire.

That was where the smell of blood was coming from! The voices. The... men.

I sniffed the air and found I could smell the odor of their flesh, sweaty and unwashed, the fats they had smeared their skin with to protect it from the wind. I could smell the animal furs they adorned their bodies with, their leather footings and the cords they tied their hair with. I could smell their cocks and their balls and their filthy, unclean asses. I could smell the hares they had eaten, the gas of their belches. But their blood... that was the strongest odor I could smell, and I wanted to fly at them and tear them to pieces and glut myself on the hot red fluid that issued forth.

I tried to move my limbs, but my limbs would not obey me.

Frustrated, I opened my eyes to see why I couldn't move.

Sight! I could see!

It was daylight, and the light stabbed into my eyes, into my brain, like two burning spears. I hissed and bared my teeth, trying to turn my head from the light, but there was no shade in which to retreat. I was trapped in that blinding glare. I felt black tears bead my eyelashes. The all-encompassing light drilled into my skull.

I snarled and snapped at the light, trying to drive it away.

Rod Redux

Bite it! Kill it!

I peeked at the world through the slits of my eyelids, maddened, furious. Slowly, then, my pupils contracted. The glare began to dim, and with that dimming, the pain it caused to me began to diminish. Sniveling, I blinked around myself, seeing without comprehending the broad rolling plains of the cold-blighted tundra in which I had awakened. I squinted up and saw ribbons of hazy, far-away clouds drifting across the blue sky. I turned my head down and saw that I lay upon a jumble of gray stones, and from the cage of my ribs there sprouted a twisted, stunted little tree, hardly more than a bush really, but it came up through the center of me, and its roots were threaded through my torso.

What is this madness?

My mind could not grasp what my eyes were reporting. I only knew that it was wrong. It hurt and it was wrong. There should be no tree screwing up through the center of me!

I tried to move my hand, to claw the small tree out of me, but my hand still refused to obey me.

I turned my attention from the bush and squinted down my shoulder to my hand. My limb, I saw, was grotesquely flattened and broken. My white flesh was fused to the gray blocks I lay sprawled across and mottled with lichen and moss. There appeared to be an unnatural number of joints throughout its length, and bones protruding from my bicep and forearm like the sharp points of broken sticks.

I tugged at my arm, but it would not move. Even my fingers were stuck, smashed flat to the stones and fused to them, unrecognizable.

I remembered then that I should have more limbs than just this one, so I looked all around for them.

My arm... where was my other arm?

Though I searched with my eyes for it, all I could see was the knob of my shoulder. I thought then to move it, or at least to try, and felt it twisted around behind my back. And my legs? Where were my legs? When I peered down my torso, I saw that my legs were submerged in the frosted earth and covered over with low grass. Here was a knee, floating in the sward like a little white island, and there, too far away from my body, the end of my foot poked up at a weird angle, my toes curled and shriveled.

Where was I? I wondered. How did I come to be this horrible, broken thing in the middle of a wind-blasted wasteland?

I tried to remember, but all I could envision was ice... an eternity of creaking white ice... pain and hunger and ice...

And the blood! The smell of blood was making me crazy! How could I get that blood? I wanted to drink it! Feel it gushing in my mouth! Gulp it down! Have it inside me!

But I couldn't move. I tried to jerk my body back and forth, but I couldn't pull free. I had become a thing of dry flesh and stone, with a tree growing up through the center of me.

Blood! Give me that blood!

Panting and snarling, my fangs protruding, I sniffed the wind blowing against my cheeks. I squinted to and fro, searching with my eyes for the source of the blood-smell.

There!

Small with distance, a party of men squatted in a circle around a low cooking fire. They were dark headed and broad, their size exaggerated by the fur-trimmed garments they clothed their bodies with. I listened to the low rumble of their chests. The sounds they were making were words, I knew, but they were words I did not understand. One of them spoke in a louder voice, and the others laughed. I counted them with my eyes—six big ones in all, with one or two small ones. I drooled as I watched them, desiring only to leap upon them, tear them apart, swallow the hot blood that squirted from the pieces. I watched them greedily, thinking only of how I might free myself stone and tree, how I might get to them so that I could feed.

I could smell the juices of the animal they were cooking over their fire. If I had been a living man, the smell of the dripping fat and sizzling flesh would have sparked my appetite, but I was no longer a living man with a living man's tastes. I was a monster, and I longed only for the blood of the hunters, not the seared meat of their prey.

I watched them hungrily all through the afternoon, hardly aware of the sun passing overhead, or the day's lengthening shadows.

Presently, one of the smaller members of their party rose to his feet and trotted away from the fire. I realized with a flash of excitement that the little one was trotting my direction.

Yes! Come, little one! Come this way!

2

I could see, with my vampire's piercing vision, that he was young and strong and pink with blood. He looked about fourteen years old, but in those ancient times that was all but a man. He had round cheeks and shaggy black hair and large, almond-shaped eyes. He came as far as halfway between his group and my position, then peered around in every direction. As I watched, he pushed aside a few layers of clothing and squatted in the grass. I watched his face redden with effort, smelled the sweet stench of his feces, then he grabbed a handful of grass, twisted it into a tuft and cleaned himself. He rose, examined his stool, and then started to return to his clan.

NO!

Thinking to tempt him nearer, I opened my jaws and made a guttural sound.

I saw him stop, his chin jerking over his shoulder in my direction. He stood stock still a moment, listening, his eyes narrowed with suspicion.

I groaned again, and saw his body stiffen with alarm. He turned fully around then and searched for the source of the noise he'd heard. His eyes swept past me, then returned. He leaned forward, squinting, and then took two steps toward me, shading his eyes with his hand.

One of the adult males in the hunting party yelled for him.

He called back to them: "*Alaie! Enong Ae!*" which meant, in his tongue, "I hear you! I'll be right there!" I did not speak their tongue until later, but that is what the words meant.

Drooling in hunger, I watched as the boy-man approached me slowly.

Yes, come closer, little one, so that I might tear my arm free of this stone and catch hold of you!

He was dressed in heavy outer furs, and beneath, a layer of woven clothes decorated with blue beading. I had never seen clothing made with such complexity, but in that animal state, I had no eye for his fashion, only for the vein throbbing in his thick, tan neck.

He crept closer and closer, then stopped, frustatingly, a good fifty meters away. He examined me with his eyes, looking up and down my form with interest.

"*Tepongoi? Ne w'ae?*"

You there, what are you?

"*Ne q'ae tsebsus?*"

Can you speak?

I twisted my torso, trying desperately to pull free. I heard my skin tear from the stones with a fibrous ripping sound, but I couldn't free myself. I couldn't get loose and catch hold of him. Furious, starved, I bared my fangs and hissed at him, and the boy-man jumped back with a horrified expression.

Without another word, he turned and pelted away.

3

Enraged, desperate with hunger, I watched the boy-man run back to his elders. Even before he rejoined them, he was motioning toward me. The men in his hunting party rose in alarm. I flung my broken white body back and forth, incensed, but I could not rip my flesh from the stones or dislodge the tree that was growing up through the center of me. I saw the boy reach the hunting party, heard the distant babble of his frightened voice. He pointed back to me emphatically, over and over, and the older men leaned down and peered in the direction he was gesturing.

Fear now was warring with my desperate hunger. I realized how foolish I had been. I was helpless, vulnerable, and now those hunters would come and they would hurt me with their spears and knives, stick me, cut me, maybe even try to burn me!

I grew more alarmed as the entire party rose and started my direction. I could see the spears and bows they carried with them. Some of them clutched knives and hatchets. One even hefted a burning branch, taking it up from the fire.

I tried to gnaw my arm, but couldn't reach it with my teeth.

They came cautiously closer, bringing their weapons to bear.

"*Ne w'ae?*" they called. "*Ne weta!*"

Closer and closer they edged, until I could make out their features, see the revulsion in their eyes. Fear and violence boiled from their pores. They recoiled in shock as they came near enough to see me clearly-- the terrible, mangled monster I'd become. Some of them fell back a step or two, and a couple of them moaned and called for my destruction in their mysterious, musical tongue.

"*Utt! Ne w'ae?*"

That, from the largest man in their group, their hunting leader or chieftain. His name was Korg, I would learn later. He was tall, dark-skinned and broad, with sleek black hair that hung down his chest on both sides of his neck, styled in thick plaits.

"*Utt! Utt!*" he prompted me.

He was dressed in ruddy reindeer fur with an ornately decorated undershirt and heavy leather leggings. Running up the right side of his face was a deep and puckered scar, a mark he'd gotten from the blow of a mammoth's tusk when he was younger and more careless. This, I would learn later, too. The scar disappeared into his hairline, from which a long stroke of gray hair wound down. He was lightly bearded but heavily muscled, with squinty grey eyes and a wide scowl of a mouth. His large hands gripped the shaft of a sturdy stone-tipped spear, which he poked in my direction as he pressed me again to answer him.

But I could not answer. Freshly awakened, I had no memories, little human intelligence. I was an animal, a broken thing with only the most basic emotions and instincts.

Frightened by my vulnerability, I displayed my fangs and snarled. *Stay away!*

My yowl frightened most of the men in the hunting party, and they fell back, moaning and gabbling. All but Korg, who did not retreat from me as the others did. Korg cocked his head to one side and then lowered his spear. He spoke to me in a softer, less urgent tone of voice, and then approached a bit closer.

I did not hiss or struggle to get free this time. I merely stared at him while he studied me.

He came closer, and then one of the other men in the party caught his shoulder, a shorter, heavy-set fellow with curly black hair and a thick frizzy beard. This one was named Lene'Hab, Korg's second-in-command. Lene'Hab had bulging and suspicious eyes, eyes that rolled my direction nervously before returning to the face of his leader. He said something low and fast, but Korg brushed his hand away and came within five meters, close enough, I noted anxiously, to pierce me with that spear.

I wouldn't know their tongue for many days, but I know now what Korg said to me as he squatted down to bargain with me that afternoon.

"I've heard of your kind before, spirit man. My father told me of the cold white ones who feed on blood," Korg said. "My father said your people have powerful magic."

It all sounded like monkey gabble to me, but later, after the boy taught me their tongue, I recalled his words and knew what he'd said.

"I will make a deal with you, white one. I will make a blood offering in your honor if you bring the mammoths back. We have hunted for nearly a moon this season and have found only their leavings. If you are as powerful a spirit as my father said, perhaps you will show us favor in the days to come."

I tried to pull free once more. I think he mistook my contortion as a nod of agreement, for he stood up then and gave a couple terse orders to the men bunched behind him. Two of the hunters bowed and ran back toward their cooking fire. Korg watched them trot away, then returned his gaze to me.

"We seal our bargain with blood, earth spirit man," he said. "Do not dishonor our agreement. My father also taught me how to send your kind to the ghost world, if the need ever arose."

I bared my fangs at him but did not hiss. I was exhausted, like a fox caught in a snare, weary of struggle.

Korg's men returned, holding two snow hares by the ears.

The Oldest Living Vampire on the Prowl

Korg thrust his spear in the ground, took the two hares in one hand. He held his other hand open and his lieutenant put the handle of a stone knife in his palm.

Korg approached carefully. I imagine his father had also warned him how dangerous the "cold white ones" could be, but the Mammoth Hunter was desperate. He had wives and children to provide for, and no mammoths to feed and clothe them with. The great wooly mammoths were nearly extinct by then, and his people's fortunes passing with them.

I eyed the hares hungrily as he approached. I had begun to grasp what he intended to do. The two hares, plump and white, wriggled their noses and kicked, but their feet were tied together with leather thongs and they could not flop free. Their bulging eyes rolled in their sockets as Korg drew near.

Korg set one aside and held the other over my head. He called out an appeal-- to me or to the spirits of his ghost world, I'm not sure which-- and then he slit the hare's throat. The furry beast squealed, its bright pink mouth gaping open, but its cry was silenced when the blade laid open its windpipe. The animal jerked as its terrified heart pumped blood from the wound in bright, pulsating arcs.

I twisted my head back, my jaws open wide. Hot, succulent blood spurted into my maw, spattered upon my dry, cracked lips. I swallowed, gasped, opened my mouth for more. I felt the demon within me leap at the nourishment, greedily encoiling the blood in my belly.

Korg squeezed the rest from the dying creature's body. He passed it back to Lene'Hab when it had finished bleeding and took up the other.

Yes! Yes! More! I swallowed the blood as fast as I could, accepting the man's sacrifice with a grateful smile. I nodded at the foreign words he spoke to me. Yes, anything you want. Just feed me!

When the second hare was drained, he gazed sternly into

my eyes. "Remember our bargain, earth spirit man," he warned me, then he turned and shooed his men back toward their camp.

At the rear of the group was a curly-headed boy. He was the smallest of them all, and slight of build, even within his heavy, layered clothing. He cast a nervous glance over his shoulder as he followed his elders away. Though I did not know it at the time, his name was Ilio, and he was about to become the last of the Mammoth Hunters… and my first vampire child.

4

A human being, on average, carries a little over five liters of blood in his body. Rabbits, of course, have quite a bit less. Korg's sacrifice only whetted my appetite, but there was enough nourishment in those three or four mouthfuls to rouse the living hunger inside me.

The Mammoth Hunters broke camp and moved on. As I watched them vanish behind a low hill, leaving me to my fate on the icy tundra, I could feel the blood of the two hares threading through my torso. The blood spread out from my belly in a web of heat and pain, repairing the destruction those dreamless ages in the glacier had wreaked on my body.

The dark hungry thing that dwells inside my kind is terribly efficient at metabolizing every drop of blood at its disposal. Even blood on the surface of the skin can be absorbed, if a vampire is starved enough. As I laid there in a stupor of pleasure and pain, I felt my cracked lips heal, the fissures sealing shut as the thing inside me knit the tissue back together. The places where the blood had dripped on my neck and face and torso turned white as all the tiny pores in my flesh sucked the nourishment in.

The hot threads meandered across my chest, into my

shoulder, then on down my right arm. Pain followed quickly after as the Strix worked to set my skin and bones in order. There was not enough blood to heal me completely, but there was enough to loosen the grip between my flesh and the stones beneath it.

With a convulsive snarl, I tore my arm free of the stones, leaving a layer of flesh behind. My limb was still twisted and broken, with dry bones jutting out, but I could wave it around a bit, and with a grimace of pain, I set my deformed fingers to work, scratching at the bark of the tree that was growing up through the center of me.

I have no idea how long I lay insensate in that remote spot, my body crushed and fused to stone, before the smell of blood aroused me. A year? A decade? A hundred years? Long enough for moss and lichen to spread across my desiccated flesh. Long enough for a tree to sprout up through my ribs.

The only true stroke of luck was that the men who found me believed me to be some kind of earthbound demi-god, and offered a blood sacrifice to me in exchange for a successful hunt.

Good luck for me... not so much for them.

I worried at that tree all through the afternoon. I could smell the humans moving further and further away as I clawed off pieces of bark. My fingers were stiff and flat and wouldn't bend very well. Bits of brittle flesh sloughed from the bones as I scrabbled at the wood. I snapped off the branches in frustration. The hunters were getting away!

I wanted their blood, not just the blood of the animals they'd snared for their dinner. I was weak, my body mangled beyond all recognition, but I pressed my crushed fingers to their task. I gave them no respite. I was ravenous. I couldn't let those hot, juicy humans escape!

As the sun descended toward the featureless horizon and the air grew ever colder, I finally managed to claw deeply enough into the heartwood of the spindly trunk to snap off the top of the tree and throw it aside. There was still a spike of jagged wood poking up through me, but I knew I would be able to push myself off it if I could free my other arm.

I began to wriggle my body back and forth until at last, beneath the purpling sky, my shoulders tore free of the stones. I snarled at the pain, jerking my torso forward again and again. Each time a little more of my flesh came off. Each time, I managed to free myself a little bit more.

I let myself rest for a while after that. To be honest, it was more of a swoon. The heat of the hares' blood had long since faded. My body was no longer repairing itself at such a frantic pace. I was exhausted and dizzy. I let my head fall back, panting. My breath made no steam in the air, as I was as cold as the stone beneath me, as cold as the permafrost in that desolate tundra.

One by one, stars began to wink in the bruised heavens above me. I remember lying there, watching them slowly appear. Those distant, blinking points of light stirred something dormant in my brain. Memories trembled at the edge of my consciousness. I could feel them there. Touch them, almost. I groped for them mentally, thinking them important for some mysterious reason… but I was still too damaged. My memories were like the smooth nub of something buried deep in the ground, and I couldn't get a grip on them. I couldn't haul them up from the frozen earth of my mind.

The Mammoth Hunters had moved beyond the range of my senses, but I knew I could still track them if I freed myself soon.

Presently, I became aware of a new source of blood. I smelled dog fur and heard the almost imperceptible beating of a distant living heart. I had begun to twist and push myself away from the stones again, but when I noticed the new blood smell, I stilled myself and probed the darkness with my potent vampire senses.

A wolf was approaching, drawn by the smell of the hares' blood the Mammoth Hunters had splattered on the ground around me.

I made myself as motionless as the stones beneath me. I could feel my blood hunger yammering inside me. *Patience!* I chastised it.

The wolf trotted out of the dark. I watched through narrowed eyes as it ambled toward me. It paused, scenting the wind, then came onwards. It was a thin, gray wolf, hardly bigger than a camp dog, its ribs showing through its mangy fur, an old bitch, exiled from her pack, perhaps. She was sick, dying. I could smell the resignation of death in her breath, in the stench of her flesh and organs.

And she could smell the blood of the hares. I heard her stomach gurgle.

But she paused again. She sensed danger.

I watched as her fear and her hunger made war. She sniffed the air. I heard her whine, low in her throat, then hunger won out over her natural wariness and she trotted forward, dipping her nose to snort at the dried blood splattered on the ground around me.

I struck.

My twisted arm shot out, faster than any striking snake, and I sank my fingers into her furry neck. The bitch leapt with a yelp, but I was far too fast. Before the animal could turn her head and snap at me with her yellow, rotting teeth, I had slashed her neck open with my fangs. I crushed her to me and drank greedily. The she-wolf's blood gushed down my throat. Her heat filled me.

Almost instantly, my flesh and bones began to knit together again. I heard a crackling sound, like dry sticks being snapped over a knee. I felt the bones in my face shift with the sound. One of the bones in my forearm drew back into the muscle, and the skin healed over.

More… I needed more!

The old wolf died, and I squeezed her body savagely to push more blood through her veins.

When I could not suck another drop from the ragged tears in the she-wolf's neck, I threw the carcass away from me. Grinning and licking my lips, I heaved my body forward and tore the rest of my fused flesh from the stones. I clawed the frozen blanket of earth from my lap to free my pelvis and upper legs. Finally free, I heaved my body onto its side, twisting myself off the wooden stake that I'd been skewered on.

I laughed then in the starlight.

Free!

My left arm was still broken and twisted around behind me, and my legs were unrecognizable, crippled and useless-- one foot was hanging by a single cord of muscle-- but I was free!

Employing my only functional arm, I began to drag myself across the frozen ground. My breath steamed now with the blood of the wolf, but it would grow cold again soon enough. My body continued to heal as I crawled like a monster across the ground, a twisted, white, crab-like thing. Fangs gleaming, eyes flashing like lamps in the dark, I crawled.

I crawled after the Mammoth Hunters, inhuman, no memory of the past and no thought of the future, just one thing in my mind: the blood-thirst, and how I might slake it.

The Last Mammoth Hunter

1

The Mammoth Hunters stalked their prey, and I stalked them.

I was curled in the scant shade of a wind-warped shrub, observing them from the pinnacle of a grassy hummock as they snuck up on the herd. It was early morning, but the light was already burning my eyes, the sun a blazing nova in the sky. I had finally caught up with hunting party after a week of crawling across the ground on my belly, and I watched them now hungrily from my hiding place, only a couple hundred meters away.

Though I'd moved without rest after freeing myself from the stones, it had taken me a week to catch up to them. The hunters moved swiftly by day. It was only at night that I managed to gain any ground on them.

My progress was slow during the day, as I had to inch forward on my belly, my face turned to the frozen ground. Contrary to popular fiction, vampires do not burst into flames at the first glint of sunlight-- ridiculous!-- but we prefer to move at night. Our eyes are very sensitive. So during the day, I slid mechanically through the grass, only faintly aware of my surroundings, following them by the scent they left behind them on the frosty earth. I made better progress at night, shuffling forward lizard-like in the dark, my eyes and fangs gleaming.

Along the way, I'd managed to catch a mole and an injured bird, and I'd sucked every drop of blood from them, but such paltry fare had done little to satisfy my hunger, or repair the horrific damage to my body. Every so often, I encountered the bones and entrails of the small animals the Mammoth Hunters had snared and devoured, and I licked the last bloody juices from the bits of offal they'd cast aside.

Each day I was able to move a little faster, until I finally caught up to the Mammoth Hunters last night.

Though I was tempted to snatch one of them from their campsite when I caught up to them, it was close to dawn and I was afraid I was too weak to kill one of them and dispose of the corpse before the sun peeked over the distant horizon. Already the eastern sky was lightening. I knew I had to wait. One of them would wander from the group tomorrow evening, I counseled my ravening thirst, and when that happened, I would be waiting. I would have the cover of darkness, and the time to do what must be done. Feed, dispose of the body and hide myself before his companions arose.

I'd followed at a distance after they roused. They made their toilet and ate before they broke camp, and now I watched them crawling forward, in the same manner I'd trailed after them, slithering through the grass on their bellies toward a small herd of mammoths.

The herd was comprised of three subordinate females and a large matriarch. There were two calves following at their mother's sides, but no bulls. Not at this time of year. The largest of the beasts, the alpha female, stood almost ten feet tall at the shoulder, and was covered, like the other adult females, in a thick and swaying shag of tangled auburn hair. The animals were tearing clods of grass from the frozen earth with their long trunks. They slapped the grass against the ground to shake the dirt from the roots, then curled their trunks under to place it in their mouths. Busy eating, none of great beasts seemed aware of the hunters winding toward them in the grass. As I watched, shading my eyes from the sun with my one good hand, I was mildly curious to see how the little men would kill one of those giant, browsing animals.

My people had encountered Mammoth Hunters from time to time when I was a living man, but I had no recollection of it then, watching them from the hill. The many millennia I'd slumbered in the glacier had pulped my brain a thousand times over, and I had not yet healed enough to recover my memories. I had become a little more cunning in the last few days, feeding on the blood of the region's scant wildlife, that and the hunters' castoffs, but that afternoon, watching the Mammoth Hunters stalk their prey, I was hardly more intelligent than any other predatory animal.

At some unseen signal, several of the hunters leapt to their feet and pelted toward the mammoths. The massive animals reared in surprise and began to thunder away from the sprinting humans. As the subordinate females fled in a panic, the matriarch of the herd doubled around, her ears flapping out to the sides in a threatening display. She moved to protect the calves at the rear of the group. The trumpeting of the shaggy animals echoed across the windy tundra.

As I watched, two of the bigger men in the hunting party ran alongside one of the smaller adult females and caught handholds in her draping pelt. They began to pull themselves up her coarse wool, hand over hand. She reared and blared as they climbed her, but couldn't jar them loose.

Korg, the leader of the hunting party, was first to haul himself onto the back of the agitated creature. He pumped one fist in the air in triumph, then reached behind to pull some kind of lance from a leather pack strapped between his shoulder blades.

Before he could stab the mammoth with his spear, the matriarch of the herd came lumbering toward him. Unlike modern elephants, both the male and female mammoth were equipped with tusks. Korg saw the matriarch's deadly tusks coming at him and swung down onto the opposite side of the smaller female's flanks. He did not drop to the ground, but clung to the beast's shaggy wool, swinging to and fro as she trampled around in fear.

The matriarch and the smaller female almost collided. The bigger mammoth trumpeted in frustration and anger, then swung away as she shifted her attention to three nearby hunters, who were chasing down a calf. Squalling in fury, she gave pursuit. Even so far away, I could feel the impact of her footsteps throbbing through the soil.

The second hunter fell off the bucking subordinate female and was struck a glancing blow by her shuffling hind leg. The impact sent him wheeling across the ground, but Korg did not fall. The big leader of the Mammoth Hunters held on.

I watched him climb back on the female's shoulders. He didn't pump his arm in triumph as he had the first time, but drove his spear into the mammoth's neck, right where the base of the animal's skull met the vertebrae of the neck. He must have missed whatever vital spot he was aiming for, however. As the female reared up, honking in pain, he grabbed two handfuls of her coarse wool and tried to cling to the bucking behemoth. His legs swung out below him. I watched, entranced, as the great beast reared, pumping her forelegs, the little man swinging back and forth from his handhold. Her feet returned to the ground with a resounding *thoomb!* then Korg regained his position, snatched another lance from his quiver and drove it into the animal's skull.

The female went down instantly, her legs buckling beneath her. The six ton beast struck the ground with a reverberating thud that made the little stones around my arm, some two hundred meters away, jump off the ground. I saw a geyser of blood jet across the hunter on her back. The sight made me twitch forward hungrily before I could restrain my appetite and hunker back down in the shade of the bush.

The alpha female glanced toward her fallen sister, then herded the others away. They receded anxiously into the distance, their mournful trumpeting and the low thunder of their movement, lingering in the air even after they'd vanished from sight.

The Mammoth Hunters gathered around the fallen cow. I watched her eyes roll round to look at them, little men jumping and pumping their fists in the air in celebration, and then she huffed and passed away.

Although there's been quite a bit of debate in recent decades concerning why the mammoths went extinct, the simple truth of the matter—at least for the wooly mammoths of the north—is that they were easy to climb onto.

I watched as the hunters began to butcher the six ton animal. A couple of the men went to tend to the fellow who was struck by the mammoth's foot. He hadn't risen from the spot where he'd rolled. The others set to the tasks of building a fire and carving into the meat of the beast.

After a few hours, the hunters settled down to palaver while mammoth steak roasted over their fire, a midday feast. One of the younger men nodded, accepting some duty they appointed him. He cut some of the sizzling meat from the spit and then turned and jogged South. Headed home, I suppose, to fetch the group's wives and children. But the young man would never complete his task. I watched him diminish into the distance, then abandoned my hiding place to trail after him.

2

The man they sent home to fetch their families was the young one who'd found me on the pile of stones, the boy-man with the shaggy dark hair. I slithered through the grass after him, falling further and further behind at first, but luckily, when he passed out of view of his elders, he quit jogging and adopted an idler pace. As the sun swung past its apex in the sky and began its slow roll westward, I found myself drawing nearer him. Near enough to smell his flesh and hear the ditty he was singing under his breath.

When he was finished eating the half-cooked mammoth meat, the boy-man stopped for a moment to piss. I slithered stealthily forward as I watched the urine arc out in front of him. He smiled to himself and swung the stream back and forth. The acrid stink of his water made me curl my nose.

I was less than a hundred meters away, but he did not sense me. Still, I approached cautiously. In my crippled condition, I knew I couldn't overtake him if he discovered me by chance.

When he was finished urinating, he looked over his shoulder the way he'd come, his almond-shaped eyes narrowed. The constant wind of the tundral steppe plucked at his lanky black hair, brushed through the fur collar of his outer clothing.

I froze where I lay, flattening my body as close as I could to the cold earth beneath me. There was little cover where I crouched, mostly lichen and moss and a few tufts of wind-bent grass.

Had he seen me from the corner of his eye? Had he heard the tiny scrapings of my movement?

No.

I smelled no alarm in his scent. After a while, I raised my

head enough to catch sight of him and found him kneeling on the ground, furiously flogging his cock. He was turned three-quarters away from me, his back hunched forward, and he was rubbing his stick like he was trying to make a fire, a breathless low groan in the back of his throat.

Grinning, I dragged myself toward him, staying low and placing my limbs carefully. I froze again when he yelped, but he was just spilling his seed. A moment later, he laced his pants and jumped to his feet. His legs were a little wobbly, but he glanced back in the direction he'd come, smiling and flushed, then continued on his way.

As the sun lowered in the sky, he gathered dry grass and shrubs while he walked, braiding them into tight bundles. I followed, and just before sunset, watched as he settled to make camp beneath the low limbs of a tree.

I observed from a distance, peeking through a gap between two exposed stones, as he retrieved his fire kit from some inner pocket in his clothing. He spread his tools out and went to work, striking two stones sharply together—flint and some iron-bearing stone. When he had his tinder smoldering, he crouched down and blew in it. After adding some larger sticks and his twisted braids of grass, he leaned back beside his crackling fire to relax. He ate some dried meat he took from a small sack tucked in his coat, then poked his fire with a stick and watching the embers swirl upwards for a while, chewing thoughtfully.

Dark came quickly once the sun dipped below the horizon. The first dim stars began to wink in the blackening sky. The boy shrugged off his coat and unfolded it, transforming his outer wear into a clever little sleeping sack, which he wrapped up in to retire for the night.

He didn't have enough kindling to keep a strong fire for long. It had burned down to coals before he'd even gotten good and asleep. The embers glowered beside him, a feeble red light, popping every few minutes as a knot or seed exploded in the heat.

The dark closed in on him.

And so did I.

I slithered nearer, then waited, twenty meters away, until his eyes drooped and he began to snore.

He didn't stir as I narrowed the distance between us. Ten meters... Then five...

I hope he was dreaming something pleasant, for it was his last night in this world.

Ordinarily, I'm hesitant to kill the young, even one as close to manhood as this boy, but I was not myself that night. Injury had robbed me of my normal compassion, as surely as it robbed me of my memories.

It shames me to describe the exhilaration with which I killed him, the pleasure I derived from drinking his life's blood, but I've sworn that I will speak no lie in the recounting of my long life. Even those acts which cast me as a villain.

He cried out when I threw myself on him, shrieking in his sudden terror like a toddling child. I threw my good arm across his head, pressing his cheek to the ground to bare his throat, and then I bit into the warm meat of his neck.

And when I say bit, I really mean "maul".

In my hunger, I savaged that poor boy. I drove my face into his neck, slashing and biting and ripping huge chunks of muscle and flesh out of him. He heaved beneath me, pushing at my head and chest for a moment, pissing in his fear, but the fight, like his life, ran out of him quickly. He collapsed beneath me with a quiet groan, his eyes rolling toward the moon before losing the spark of awareness.

I sucked the blood out of him as quickly as I could, for it would not spurt as forcefully when his heart stopped beating. He died and then I pumped down on his chest, trying to force as much blood out of him as possible.

I rose up on my knees, feeling the heat of his life surging through me. I moaned and threw my head back as the bones of my face shifted, realigned.

My injuries healed rapidly. My left arm finally came free of my back and dropped down by my side. My dangling foot drew back to the mangled stump of my ankle, reattaching. My right arm snapped and popped, becoming the arm of a man again, smooth skinned and with only the natural joints and bulges.

I licked the blood from my lips, my fingers, my forearms. Turning back toward the boy, I stripped away his furs and underclothes until he was naked beneath me, then I dropped upon him and began to bite into his flesh. I gnawed at him like a starved wolf would gnaw at the bones of a reindeer, slashing him in a thousand different places to suck the last dregs of his blood from the capillaries of his skin. I gutted him, pulling his organs from the cage of his ribs, then licked the juices from his tangled entrails. Finally, I plucked out his heart and ate it raw.

Kneeling there beneath the stars, with the boy-man's blood smeared all over my hands and chest and face, I cried out in the dark.

"I am Gon! I still live!"

3

For the first time in seven thousand years, I had a man's shape; I had a man's voice. For the first time in seven thousand years, I spoke as a man spoke.

But my name was all I knew.

I sat down beside the corpse of the young Mammoth Hunter and tried to recall my past. Though I could sense memories trembling at the edge of discovery, there was still a vast gulf of darkness separating me from my recollections.

"I am Gon," I said hoarsely. "But who is Gon?"

I looked toward the mangled corpse beside me, but my victim could be no help to me.

"Who are you?" I asked him, then gazing all around, "And where am I? What is this cold and barren place?"

My face knuckled up as I put my questions to the starry heavens.

I placed my fingertips to my features and explored them, running my touch through my disheveled hair, then down to the jutting cliff of my brow, the bony bridge of my nose with its soft bulbous tip, then finally on below to my broad and sensual mouth, rimmed by wiry tufts of mustache and beard. Who am I? It troubled me intensely that I could not recall the image of my own face. There was no pool of water nearby in which to gaze. I thought, maybe if I saw my own face, I would remember myself. Maybe I would remember who this "Gon" fellow was. I decided I would look on my reflection the first opportunity I got.

But for now...

For now I would walk as a man walks. No more crawling in the grass like a snake.

I looked down my body in the moonlight, admiring the shape of it. No longer mangled, no longer broken, it was smooth and white in the lunar light.

There were still blemishes and a couple places where the bone showed through gaps in the flesh, but I looked like a man again. There beneath me was a man's feet, a man's hairy legs, a man's cock and balls (my organ standing rigidly at attention, I must confess; that happens a lot when male vampires glut themselves on blood, a little something you might not know... or want to know!).

My hands glittered in the silver light. I tried to brush away the sparkles, thinking them frost perhaps, or some dusting of stone flecks, but I soon realized the winking was actually a quality of my white, smooth flesh. My skin was not soft and tan like the skin of the dead boy, but of some inscrutable material that seemed porous and unnatural.

The joints of my hands popped a little when I squeezed them into fists. I studied them as I turned my palms and flexed the fingers, and for just an instant I remembered carving a little deer out of wood for one of my children, holding it up in these hands to examine it before passing it on to my grasping son.

My son...!

Excited, I tried to picture the boy's face. I tried so hard my forehead furrowed, but the image would not come. I felt my eyes grow moist and I scrubbed them angrily.

"Where are you, son? What is your name?" I whispered. "Are you still alive? Are you waiting for me to come home?"

If I had a son, I reasoned, then I must also have a wife, but I could not summon her visage either.

The blood inside me was cooling now. My flesh began to wither and grew chill. I watched a mist rise off the surface of my skin as my body temperature dropped, then turned my face toward the North, my eyelids narrowing down to greedy slits.

If I had more blood, then perhaps I would remember!

My hunger stirred, restless, greedy. Pangs of agony coiled and struck the inside of my belly, a nest of angry snakes. I observed my flesh draw tight to the bone. My cock drooped and shriveled as the dark thing inside me—the Living Hunger, the Venom-- used up the last of the Mammoth Hunter's blood. I cast my gaze down to the murdered boy-man. His clothes were shredded and stank of his strung out guts. No, I could not wear those things! Better to be naked. Besides, the cold seemed to have no effect on me. I could feel it, but it did not pain me. It did not make my muscles quake.

But I must have more blood!

I turned northward and began to limp toward the camp of

the remaining Mammoth Hunters. I could not run. I could not lift myself from the earth in great bounds, but at least I was no longer crawling on my belly in the dust.

I walked for a couple hours in the dark, until I'd drawn near their camp again, then squatted down outside the glow of their leaping orange fire. They were making quick work of the mammoth, I saw. Some of its hide was already staked out to be scraped and tanned later by their women.

All but two men were wrapped up in their sleeping rolls, snoring. There were two hunters on watch, guarding their kill from any hungry scavengers that might be bold enough to sneak into the camp by night. They were sitting by the fire, talking quietly, their spears thrust in the dirt.

I pondered how I might snatch one of them without alerting the others. The hunger inside me was an agony.

On the far side of the camp, a wild dog cried out.

The guards grabbed their spears and rose, blinking into the darkness. One of them took a braided paddle-like contraption and shook it toward the shadows. Some kind of noise-maker. The animal yipped and whined but did not approach the light. After a while, the men relaxed and sat back down, putting their weapons aside.

It was not long before one of them began to nod. His partner gestured for him to lie down and rest. I leaned forward, excited, as the first man curled up in his furs to sleep. There was just one man awake now. An old one, by the smell. Could he stay awake much longer? I rose to a crouch and crept a little bit closer.

He caught the flash of my eyes in the dark! I'd forgotten how reflective my pupils were. I saw the old hunter turn with a start and he probed the dark around me with his gaze, plucking his spear from the ground.

Quickly, before he caught sight of me, I dropped to the ground and squeezed my eyes to slits.

He pushed upright, hands on his knees, and weaved his way through the other sleeping hunters to look for me. He stared very near where I lay.

I was starting to think he could actually see me when his shoulders slumped and he returned to the fire.

I waited.

At last the old man nodded off, his chin to his chest, and I slipped through the dark to the hunter lying furthest from the fire. Clamping my hand over his mouth, I twisted his head violently to one side. His eyes flashed open but it was too late. I opened his arteries with my fangs and began to feed, even as I dragged the thrashing man into the dark.

His heart was strong and hot blood sprayed into my mouth-- a coppery flood. He pulled at the hand clamped to his mouth. Kicked his feet. A couple of the others stirred in their sleep as my victim writhed and clawed at the earth with his fingers, but I had strength enough to steal him away undiscovered.

I drained the man under the moonlight and then lay back on the ground beside him, lacing my fingers over my heart. I sighed contentedly, feeling his blood coursing through me. Looking up at the sky, I realized I once believed those points of light to be the spirits of my forefathers. I recalled my father saying they were the campfires of those who'd passed into the spirit world. I turned to the man lying beside me, excited by this reclaimed memory.

"I remember now, Brulde! Those lights in the heavens are the spirits of our grandfathers," I said, but then I realized the man beside me was dead. Who was this Brulde I'd spoken to? Why did his name come unbidden to my thoughts?

Who are you, Brulde? I wondered, sitting upright.

I put my hands to my head, squeezing my temples in frustration.

Brulde, Brulde, Brulde... and Eyya, my wife! I could

picture her face in my mind suddenly. The blood of the Mammoth Hunter was healing my brain.

My woman's name was Eyya! She had large brown eyes and dark coarse hair, which she braided with gleaming blue and black feathers. I remembered how her skin glowed in the sunlight, for she loved to paint her flesh with gold ochre. She thought it made her pretty, and it had.

I remembered her pushing me into the soft warmth of our sleeping furs, her hands on my shoulders. "Rest now, husband. Let me comfort you tonight," she murmured, smiling down at me. I watched her full breasts swing above my mouth. Oh, how I wanted to wrap my lips around those big, crinkled nipples, suckle at her bosom like a baby! But not tonight. Tonight she was the sucking one. I gulped as she unlaced my leggings and freed my stiffening worm.

I remembered Eyya, her face sweaty and straining, as she squatted over the birthing pit I'd dug and lined with rabbit skin, her strangled cry as our first child swelled out of her maidenhood, spilled moistly into the furs. I was so overwhelmed, I almost fainted. Eyya fell back on her bottom, exhausted, the umbilical cord trailing from between her thighs, and I scooped our baby from the birthing pit and cleared his little mouth with my finger. With trembling hands, I cut the cord and tied it with a length of string.

"Look, beloved! It's our baby!" I said, laughing and crying at the same time, and then the tiny thing wrinkled up his purple face and started to wail. So loud! Such a strong little boy!

"I want to name him after my father," I said, weeping proudly, and Eyya nodded.

The memories were so powerful, they swept me to my feet. Where are you, Eyya? I wondered, turning in a circle. I wanted to fly back home to her, but I did not know where I was!

I had to remember more. I had to remember my way back to my family!

I returned to the camp of the Mammoth Hunters that night and took one more.

My strength and the speed of my movements were growing exponentially. In my ignorance, I marveled at my powers, and at the rapid restoration of my body. Even the places where bone was showing before had vanished, the flesh growing over the wounds.

I slashed through the undulating grassland, quick as the wind. Quicker. My third victim's neck snapped like a dry stick when I dragged him to my fangs. He didn't have time to thrash or cry out like the other. I fed on him like a starved wolf, and then I dragged the two bodies away and hid them from their companions.

Daylight was fast approaching. I could see its radiance on the horizon, the low clouds glowing purple and pink along the rim of the desolate steppe. I was tired. My belly was full-- sloshing even, with the contents of my victim's veins. The blood was not being utilized as quickly as it had before, and like any living man with a straining stomach, I only wanted to sleep, but I dragged the bodies behind me without slowing. I knew I must hide them before I allowed myself to rest. The why was not important. It was an instinctive urge.

I carried the two bodies a good distance away before I searched out a place to hide myself for the day. I felt I needed to conceal the evidence of my predations, and myself, from the men I hunted. I still did not yet remember the measure of my powers, and I feared vulnerabilities there was no need to worry about.

If I was in full possession of my mind, I would not have feared the retaliation of the Mammoth Hunters, but though some of my memories had been restored, I was still very ignorant of my past and my superhuman vampire attributes.

Rod Redux

As the first blazing wedge of the sun flashed over the distant plains, I wriggled into a crevice in the earth, a narrow cleft that running water had carved alongside a dry creek bed. It was out of sight and just barely deep enough to conceal my whole body. Still I was pretty sure I'd travelled far enough from the campsite of the Mammoth Hunters. I didn't think they would stumble across me as they looked for their missing companions.

I slept with my face turned toward the dark. Though I could feel the sun on my back, my bare flesh tightening with the heat, the darkness inside the crevice was cool and comforting, and my grip on wakefulness soon loosened. Dirt trickled on my cheek as I closed my eyes. Dangling roots tickled my nose. My mind cast adrift like a leaf on a stream. Soon after, I dreamed.

Yes, vampires dream.

Our sleep is very deep, and alternates between passages of death-like insensibility and vivid dreams. My memories were returning, and my dreams that morning were shot through with flashing fragments of my human life in the valley of the Swabian Alb. I dreamed of my early childhood, a son of the River People. I dreamed of my mother, who died when I was young, and I dreamed of my father, whom I idolized, the mighty hunter Gan. I dreamed of my older brothers. I dreamed of our crowded wetus, and playing tag with the child who would one day become my tent mate, my blonde-headed cousin Brulde.

I dreamed of the Fat Hands, and how they came down to the river to catch fish and bathe. I was a little boy in that dream. The hulking Neanderthal men seemed so big and fascinating. I loved to watch them wade out naked in the river. Someday I will be as big and strong as them, I thought to myself. I waded into the river to help them, pulling the fish from their spears when they caught them.

The Oldest Living Vampire on the Prowl

The Neanderthals laughed at me and called me Little Worm in their deep, resounding voices. "Here, Little Worm! Get this fish off my spear for me!" Stodd, the towering patriarch of the Fat Hand fishers, yelled after me. His massive, hairy body rippled with muscle. "Quick! Don't let it flap off!" His teeth flashed broad and white within the tangles of his bushy red beard.

I dreamed of the day our village was raided by the Foul Ones, the tribe of flesh-eaters that resided to the north of our valley. They were men like us, but despicable and depraved. They stole our women and children. They raped. They murdered. They ate the flesh of their own kind, and wore the bones as ornamentation. My father had rescued me from one of the strange invaders just as the marauder was about to scoop me into his arms and steal me away.

The monster who made me a vampire hailed from those same cruel people, or so I believed. He sharpened his teeth like they did, and wore human bones as decoration. I dreamed of him flying down into the charnel pit where he had imprisoned me, his furs spreading out like the wings of a great bird of prey. He landed in a crouch and stalked toward me, and I scrambled away across the stiff, frozen bodies of all the Neanderthals he had devoured and discarded. His eyes flashed red in the shadowed pits beneath his brows. His lips split open to reveal what looked like a hundred sharpened teeth. He was coming to kill me… He was coming to steal my life away!

Dreaming of the fiend who made me a vampire, I jolted awake. For a moment, I wasn't sure where I lay, only that it was dark and I was enveloped in the smell of raw soil. For just a second, I thought I was back in the charnel pit where I had been transformed into a blood-drinker, and, panicking, I began to claw at the earthen cavity surrounding me.

I spilled out of the narrow channel of dirt and rolled onto

my back. Lying there in the dry wash, the grass overhead swaying in the wind, I saw the moon and stars, and realized it was all just a dream, that I had slept through the day, undiscovered, and night had returned.

Hunger squeezed my guts. I was cold, starving.

I rose naked in the starlight and reached out with my senses. There, to the north: the Mammoth Hunters. They hadn't abandoned their camp. Not yet. I could smell their warm bodies, hear the murmur of their voices, even at such a great distance.

With a wicked grin, I leapt from the dry creek bed and went to hunt.

4

I took their leader Korg that night.

There were five left by then: Korg and his second-in-command Lene'Hab, an old hunter named Elk, a young man named Hammon and the boy-child Ilio. None of them were sleeping when I returned to the camp. They all stood guard around a blazing fire, watching the outer darkness with their weapons clutched tight in their fists.

I could smell their fear as I circled the camp. I kept a far enough distance that they did not see the flash of my eyes or hear the sound of my movements. The blood of their brothers had healed my body. I moved like a wraith in the moonlight, blurring from one vantage to another, probing for weakness, waiting for an opportunity to strike.

Though much of my past was still a mystery to me, my mind had healed enough that I remembered my powers, and I took full advantage of them. In fact, I reveled in them.

I watched, and when Korg stepped away from the fire to piss after an hour or so, I snatched him away. He only took a few steps from the safety of the group, but it was enough.

The Oldest Living Vampire on the Prowl

The speed at which I bolted toward him rendered me invisible to their gaze. It's not a hard trick to pull off for a vampire like me, especially at night. The men standing guard would have seen less than a blur. To their eyes, it would have looked like had Korg simply melted into darkness.

The force that struck the man as I flew down and snatched him from his feet knocked him unconscious. I bound into the air with the unconscious Mammoth Hunter in my arms, the cold tundral wind blasting across my cheeks. I could hear his companions crying out in horror and confusion behind me, but I ignored their loud dismay. My mind was not yet whole. Because of that, I was no more compassionate than the beast who made me a vampire. I thought only of the need inside me. The Hunger, and its satiation.

I landed with a thump and threw the unconscious Mammoth Hunter on the ground. My violent abduction had bruised him. His fine beaded clothes hung from his limbs in tatters. His flesh was purpling where my fingers had sunk into him. Blood trickled from one nostril.

I leered as his eyelids fluttered, my mouth watering for him, my fangs exposed. He stirred, then opened his eyes and looked at me, confused. Seeing my sharp-toothed grin, he scrambled away with a cry.

How cruel I was with him that night! How like my maker! It shames me to recount it.

The Mammoth Hunter named Korg was a brave man. After scrambling out of my reach, the burly hunter vanquished his fear and pulled a stone blade from his breeches. He leapt to attack me, uttering a warrior's cry, a deep-chested challenge. Laughing in mockery, I grabbed his wrist and snapped the bones in his forearm. His blade tumbled from his spasming fingers as bony shards breached his flesh, a bloody eruption. He howled in agony, clutching his broken arm, and I stepped toward him and knocked him to the ground. He shouted as I fell upon him, striking my ribs and my back with his fist. I pushed his chin up with my head. My jaws stretched wide. With one quick lunge, I bit into the flesh of his throat.

But not too deeply--!

I wanted to relish this kill. Holding his head by his hair, I fed on him. Slowly. I savored every spurt. I gulped and sighed. In his last moment, his fist flattened out on my back and it was almost like he embraced me... embraced death. The Mammoth Hunter murmured something softly. I'm not sure what it was. I was too enraptured in the feeding. He sighed, and then his heart fell still. His palm slid down my smooth white back, lifeless, and then his arm rolled into the grass.

I fed upon him a while longer, then I reluctantly withdrew my fangs from him. I rose to my feet and swayed, my body flushed and tingling, my cock engorged. I wiped the blood from my lips and chin with the back of my arm and then licked the blood from that, too.

I was tempted to return to the camp and take another. I might have done it, if not for the memories crowding in my skull.

My head throbbed with the hunter's blood. I could feel it inside me, repairing the cells of my brain.

Flashes of my former life—Nyala, sweeping aside the flap of our wetus, young but imperious, demanding that we take her as a wife. Eyya, embracing Brulde and I in the reeds beside the river. Eyya and Nyala both, laughing so hard they had to cling to one another to stand as Brulde and I bounced around our tent, all six of our children riding on our backs. I remembered Brulde looking at me and laughing as we squatted beside a campfire. We were eating venison, the two of us out hunting in the mountains, as a light snow drifted down around us.

Overwhelmed, I staggered away in the dark.

Nyala, fighting with her sisters. Eyya, suckling our babies

by the fire. Brulde, practicing with his bow.

Where are you?

I tripped and fell. Eyes squeezed shut, I crawled on my hands and knees.

Brulde and I, naked in the river, splashing with our sons in the sunshine, scrubbing them with silty mud. Our group family, tangled in our sleeping furs, making love. All the babies asleep. Slick, warm flesh under my lips, in my hands, sliding tight and wet upon my cock.

I think I knew it then, where they were, what was past and what was present... but I could not accept it. My heart cowered from the revelation. I shook my head, trying to deny it, but there it was, in all its horror. The truth. The rest of my lost memories. I fell on my face and clawed at the earth and grass beneath me. My cheeks were wet with tears.

Dead. They were all dead. A hundred years dead. A thousand years dead.

No! I thought, shaking my head. *No, they're still alive! They're waiting for me to come home!*

I rolled onto my side, still denying, still shaking my head. I brought my knees to my chest and wrapped my arms around them.

5

"Imagine the pain," I said to the man duct taped to the chair in my apartment. "You wake with no memories. You don't know where you are. You don't even know who you are. Your body is smashed beyond all recognition. You are crippled. Monstrous. But then a miracle occurs. You are healed. One by one, your memories return, and they are good memories, memories of love and pleasure. You are excited, overjoyed. You see a path that leads back home, back to the loved ones waiting there for you, their arms open in welcome.

"And then you realize, like the fictional character Rip Van Winkle, that the world has passed you by while you slept.

"I did not return to my valley. I never have. Not in the flesh. I return to it in my memory. I return to it again and again, even now, thirty millennia later. I watch them from afar, much like I did so long ago, when I was first transformed into a vampire. I watch from afar as my beautiful wives and my quiet, enduring husband grow old and die. I wish I had gone to them then, cold and white and evil as I am, but I did not—I could not—return to their side. I had become a monster, and I did not trust myself to resist the lure of their warm, nourishing blood. I retreated to a cave like a monster in a fairy tale and watched them from a distance, undying, ageless, and now I remembered it all. Lying there in the tundra, my memories tortured me.

"I remembered how time took my lovers from me, one by one, how I flew down to the village and collected their remains. By then, the people of the river called me Thest-Un-Mann, which meant "the ghost who is a man" and I brought their bodies, one by one, to the cave to keep me company. I buried them there, and with me they remained, for decades, for hundreds of years, I do not know how long I resided there, but they were my only companions through that long epoch of self-imposed exile. I was the ultimate hermit. God of the recluses. I only left my mountain when disaster threatened my people.

"I remembered the ages that passed, as my children and my children's children grew up and then succumbed to time. I remembered how the world grew cold and my people forsook our valley, how the glaciers spilled over the northern mountains until all that remained was ice, and when I could bear my solitude no longer, I went down to that ice and cast myself into a deep and lightless crevasse.

"There was no going home, I realized. Everything I knew was dust. The ones I'd loved the most were ancient bones in a distant and long abandoned cavern.

"I mourned them afresh, lying in that distant tundral steppe. I cried for them all through the night. The pain accompanied me even into the daylight hours that followed, as I slept in the shallow fissure in the dry creek bed. I dreamed of Eyya and Brulde and Nyala, and woke with my vile black tears crusted upon my cheeks.

"I took the young Mammoth Hunter named Hammon that night.

"I found the survivors many miles away, having abandoned their camp. They were fleeing home. They were jogging south through the starlight when I caught up to them.

"I took Hammon from their ranks without a sound and dressed myself in his clothes after draining his body of blood.

"Ashamed of my gluttony, I decided to spare the boy and the wizened old man. I had come, at last, to think as my true self, with all my mind intact.

"Yes, I would let the boy and the old man live. I was not like the monster who had made me into a vampire.

"With no home to return to, and no glacier to throw myself in, I started walking south, parallel to the two surviving Mammoth Hunters. I was not stalking them. South merely seemed as good a direction as any other, and their distant presence was comforting to me."

6

When I woke the following evening, the sun a squashed and bloody thing in the western sky, the constant wind of the steppes carried to my sensitive ears the sound of a child's weeping. Feeling ashamed that I had wrought such terror and deprivation on another soul, I turned my back to that distant lamentation and ordered my legs to carry me away. There was nothing I could do to atone for my crimes, not to this group of unlucky hunters-- save to spare the survivors any further harm.

But after a few steps, I faltered. Why was the boy crying so inconsolably? Why was his voice the only voice I heard riding on the wind?

Reluctantly, I turned and followed the sound of his grief.

I found the crying child sitting beside the old man. The boy's legs were crossed, his head hanging. I crouched to look at him, watched his shoulders tremble up and down as he mourned the fallen elder.

The ancient Mammoth Hunter was lying on his back in the grass. Even from a distance, I knew the old man had passed on to the afterlife. The ancient one's body was cold and gray. His eyes were rolled up in their sockets. No steaming breath stirred the chill night air from his blue and unmoving lips.

Yes, he was gone, and out of love, the child had folded the old man's arms across his chest, lingering to weep at his side, one of his hands placed lightly on the old man's belly.

Even as I felt pity for the boy-child, my appetite for his blood gnawed at me.

You should go, I counseled myself. *Better to leave him to his fate than tempt your blood-lust with his company.*

I knew he would not survive any attempt on my part to assist him. Eventually, my hunger would win out, and I would take him.

Yet, either way he would die, I argued with myself. Look at him! He cannot survive here in this cold and desolate waste. With no elders to look after him, he was doomed. Isn't it better to make the attempt and fail than to slink away like a coward?

I don't know why I went to him. I don't know whether my motivation was pity or guilt. Perhaps I was simply lonely, having realized I had no wives and children to return to.

I try to be noble, but I am a selfish creature at heart, so perhaps I desired a companion with whom to share my pain and loneliness with. It was probably a stew of all those motives, but regardless of the reasons, I finally went to him.

But before I did, I took a handful of earth and rubbed it on my shining flesh. I did not want him to know I was the fiend who'd taken his family from him. The single time the boy laid eyes on me, I was a crushed and hissing monster, fused to stone with a tree growing out the middle, an inhuman thing, a fearsome earth spirit. I had healed, but I did not want to startle him with my twinkling white flesh. I wanted him to think I was a man who'd crossed his path by coincidence. He was young. He would accept my arrival as good fortune.

As I approached in the moonlight, I whistled a quiet tune, giving him time to hear me. I walked as a man walked, thinking cleverly to pass near the boy, not come at him directly.

I heard his weeping fall silent. I heard him listen to my whistling. He'd gone as still as a hare, fearful of the fox, waiting in terror, I'm sure, for some demon to come flying out of the dark to claim him.

I passed him at a distance and continued on. As I passed, I hummed a song I once sang for my children. It was a song about young rabbits playing in a field, seeing who could hop the highest. It was one of my kids' favorite songs. Whenever I sang it, they would scramble to their feet and start hopping, trying to out-jump one another.

After a short distance, I stopped and gathered tinder to make a campfire. It was a quick, easy chore. I had no flint to make sparks, so I found a couple pieces of wood to rub together. I employed a bit of my superhuman speed and the wood promptly burst into flames. Not my best trick, but gratifying. I built the fire up as large as I could, using what wood I could scrounge in the immediately vicinity, and even

Rod Redux

some freeze-dried mammoth piles. They were good, if redolent, fuel.

After a while, I sensed the boy approach. I heard his cautious movements as he circled my fire.

Smiling pleasantly, I sang another song my children once favored, a song about a magic deer that jumped into fires to feed hungry children. The smell of the boy's blood was tempting. I wanted chase him down and chew his neck open, but the blood of my last kill was still warm inside my flesh, and I was able to wrestle the blood-thirst down. It was actually a little easier than I thought it would be, now that I had made the decision to fight it.

I could hear his breathing, the rapid beating of his heart.

After a time, I curled up near the fire and feigned sleep.

It was good to lie near a fire as a man would lie. The brisk wind of the steppes tossed the flames of my campfire one direction and then another. The tongues the fire flapped and twisted. Sparks spun away into the night sky, orange embers, flaring for just an instant before dying away.

I watched the flames whip. I watched the moon creep slow as a snail from one end of the heavens to the other. Moonlit clouds drifted, restlessly changing shape, like foam in the rapids. I finally did sleep then, like a real mortal man. I dreamed I was a boy, helping the Neanderthals fish near the bank of our river in the valley. The big Fat Hand Stodd was there, my youthful hero, so strong and careful of me. I was just a little boy from a neighboring tribe, no kin of his, but he always treated me kindly, and he never let me come to harm. "Grab it quick, Little Worm, before it flaps away!" he called to me.

I snapped awake as the boy approached.

I heard the whisper of his feet in the grass. The thud of his heart. I smelled the fear in his sweat.

I didn't move. I lay as if in slumber.

Finally, he called to me in the tongue of his people. *"Utt! Ne n'ghoi? Utt!"*

I sat up abruptly, as a mortal man would sit up, startled from his sleep. Though I knew exactly where the boy stood, I pretended to blink into the surrounding darkness, confused and a little frightened. I'd picked up some of his people's language in the last few days, so I called out in his tongue: *"Ne w'ae? Ne st'oh?"* which roughly translated as: "Who is it? Who's there?"

The boy crept into the circle of dancing firelight, pointing a spear at me. He was small, thin, with a round face and large, worrisome eyes. It was probably those eyes which preserved his life in the days that followed. They reminded me tremendously of the eyes of my companion Brulde. Large and slightly bulging, a blue-gray color, and full of nervousness, always looking out at the world as if something large and hungry was about to pounce.

And who knows? Maybe this boy-child was a descendant of my companion Brulde? Our people had abandoned our valley when the glaciers returned, so very, very long ago. Perhaps Brulde's descendants had flourished, even while I slept in my tomb of ice.

It was certainly possible this boy was a great-to-the-nth-degree grandchild, that our progeny had bred with the Mammoth Hunters. I did not know what became of our descendants after they abandoned the valley.

Not then, anyway.

I put my hands up, showing him my empty palms, then nodded apprehensively toward his weapon.

Seeing my unease, the boy lowered his spear. He said something I did not understand.

I shook my head, lowered my hands. I looked him up and down sympathetically.

"What's your name, boy?" I asked, in the tongue of the

River People. "Are you cold? Come, warm yourself by the fire."

The boy narrowed his eyes, watching me warily. He didn't understand the language of the River People, didn't like my foreignness.

I smiled and gestured for him join me by the fire, which he did, but his big, careful eyes didn't stray from me for a moment, and he sat well out of my reach, the shaft of his spear lying across his thighs. He pulled the fur-lined gloves he wore off his hands and held his palms up near the fire. His hands, I saw, were trembling from the night chill.

"Thest-Un-Mann," I said, tapping my chest.

He stared at me fretfully, then his shoulders fell and he tapped his chest and said, "Ilio."

I smiled again, careful not to expose my fangs. "Thest-un-Mann. Ilio." Gesturing from me to him.

He finally smiled-- faintly, hesitantly-- back at me, then repeated my gesture. "Ilio. Thest-un-Mann."

I chuckled and nodded. There was not much else we could say to one another. Though vampires are quick at adopting unfamiliar dialects, my mind had not been my own those first few days I was stalking the Mammoth Hunters. I was little more than an animal until the cursed blood repaired my mind. I had paid little attention to the sounds the hunters grunted at one another. For now, we were divided by ignorance, and could only sit and eye one another suspiciously.

I gestured that I was lying back down and he nodded, still warming his hands by the fire. I lay on my side and watched him across the fire. The terror that sprang to his eyes every time a sound arose in the darkness made me feel very ashamed. I was the cause of that fear. I had killed all his companions save one, the old man, and the ancient hunter Elk had probably died because of me as well, their fearful flight overtaxing his ancient heart. Now here I was, lying on the ground across the fire from the boy, a deceiver as well as a destroyer. Could I ever atone for so many offenses?

The boy slowly relaxed. He took off his outer coat and made a sleeping roll for himself and wrapped up in it. He lay down as if to sleep, but his wide eyes rolled at every sound, and he trembled long after the fire should have warmed him.

Monster, I accused myself, watching him through the leaping flames. *You are worse than the Foul One who made you!*

After a little while, I began to sing again. I sang the song of the deer that jumps in the fire. It is a sweet and soothing song, a kind of lullaby. I'd sung it to my children many times as I sat cross-legged by the fire, rocking them in my arms and brushing their hair from their brows. Little Gan. Little Breyya. Little Hun. All my children. I remembered how their eyes would glaze over in sleepiness, then roll back in their sockets, their little thumbs in their mouths.

As I sang my people's lullaby song, the boy Ilio relaxed, and then his eyes drifted closed. He slept as my children once slept, his eyes slightly open, little crescents of white showing between the lashes.

I fell in love with him a little, seeing him drift off to sleep as my children once had. I swore to myself that very night, I would keep this child safe… at any cost.

It was a promise I did not keep.

7

After the boy fell asleep, I rose silently and stole from the camp. The blood-hunger was clamoring in my belly, and I feared my resolve. I hunted the dark tundra, seeking my evening meal of the region's wildlife, as I had done in the past when I watched over the River People from my mountain refuge.

I flew in great leaps and bounds, my hair streaming out behind me, and came across a small herd of reindeer gathered by a frosted pool. The animal I took was large and full of blood. As its herd thundered away, I tore open its neck and drank until my belly was quivering, then I used my superhuman strength to rip away its haunch, which I carried back to the fire with me. I planned to cook the loin for the boy in the morning, when he awoke.

Feeling more sure of myself, I got comfortable by the fire and waited for sunrise to come. It would be uncomfortable for me to move about in daylight. The light would sting my eyes. But for his sake, I would do it. Watching him sleep across the fire from me, I felt a great swell of protectiveness rise up in my heart for him.

I had done so much to harm him, but no more.

Ilio... so small and fragile, more child than man. This hunt was surely the first expedition he'd gone on. To my way of thinking, he hardly seemed big enough to leave his mother's side. None of the men I'd stalked had seemed particularly mindful of the child, as a father should be. He'd seemed more a tagalong than anything else. Perhaps he was an orphan and was being raised by the hunting men in his tribe.

The boy slept through the night as I watched over him. When dawn broke, I built up the fire and spit the deer haunch over it.

Ilio slept until full daylight, then rose up with a lurch, confused and frightened. He blinked at the steppes surrounding us on all sides as if he could not believe he'd lived to see another day.

I smiled and nodded at him, pointing at the deer meat roasting over the fire. I rubbed my belly and licked my lips in an exaggerated manner.

Ilio smiled back shyly. He sat up in his furs, his curly dark hair smashed flat on one side and sticking up in spikes on the other. His face was puffy with sleep, his eyes red and swollen.

I tore off a hunk of steaming meat and passed it to him. He murmured something in his alien tongue and ate hungrily, smacking his lips and then licking the grease from his fingers when it was gone. He looked at me imploringly, speaking some more words I did not understand, but I recognized the tone of his speech and gave him a second helping.

He was much happier when his belly was full. For a while, we played the game of naming things, learning one another's language. He pointed to the fire and said, "Stoh," and I mimicked him, saying the River People word for it: "Echah." He pulled up a hank of grass. "Sah." I patted the grass. "Ess" I ignored the pain stabbing in my eyes from the sunlight as we continued with the naming game. The word for sky was "enghoi". That bird flying there in the enghoi was called "creewah". My mind held onto every word he taught me. Vampires retain information very easily. The dark blood inside us preserves our memories in much the same manner that it preserves our flesh, I suppose.

After an hour, he said he needed to do something I didn't understand. I watched as he rose and walked away from the fire a little ways.

He didn't move too far away. I think he was worried the monster who'd killed his companions would try and get him if he went too far. He looked all around and then, keeping an eye on me nervously, he pulled out his little boy penis and began to urinate.

Ah! That's what that word meant! "T'sitz"!

He finished quickly and returned to the fire. I fed him some more and we continued with the naming game as we rose and put out the fire and gathered our belongings.

He pointed south and said, "I want/need to—something-something." I shrugged and nodded and we began to walk south.

Rod Redux

He latched onto me quickly, as children are wont to do. By nightfall, I'd learned enough of his tongue that we could maintain a basic dialogue.

He was still fearful that first day. Even as we walked further and further south, his eyes roved to and fro without cease, scanning our surroundings for the monster who'd killed his companions. When he needed to void his bowels, he strayed only a little distance, and he watched me the whole time to make sure I didn't turn my eyes away from him. The rest of the day, he stayed within arm's length. He even gave me his spear to carry. I'm a tall, broad-shouldered man. Perhaps he believed I was big enough to protect him if the monster attacked us.

As the sun began to set, he clung even closer to me. Almost underfoot. We gathered tinder together for our fire, speaking haltingly.

"There... get stick," I said.

"Okay."

"Let's make fire now."

I gave him the rest of the meat when night fell, which he devoured ravenously. We made a big fire, but he sat right beside me anyway, staring out at the dark with barely concealed terror.

His fear shamed me afresh. I listened and nodded solemnly as he tried to explain the terrible things that had befallen his hunting party, the monster who had stalked and killed his family. I did my best to comfort and reassure him, though I was hesitant to touch him more than necessary. I was afraid he would notice the chill of my flesh, its horrid and inhuman texture.

So far he had displayed no suspicion that I was anything more than a living man. If he noticed the pallor of my skin, or the strange way my eyes glinted, he gave no sign of it. It was the dark he feared, or more exactly, the monster he imagined in the dark, the misshapen thing he'd seen squashed to the rocks.

But I was growing hungry as well. My appetite for blood was mounting with the night. His nearness tortured me. I'm ashamed to say, the smell of his blood made my mouth water. I sat stiffly beside him, afraid I would lose control of myself if I touched him. I couldn't bear the thought of harming him.

He put my self-control to the test, however, when it came time to sleep. He insisted we lie next to one another near the fire, shaking his head stubbornly when I gestured for him to sleep apart from me.

"Please," he begged, "I'm afraid it will get me. It comes at night." His eyes were so large and terrified, I could do nothing but acquiesce to his wishes.

We lay down side-by-side under the stars. He asked me to do something I didn't understand. Then, when he tapped his lips and made a humming sound, I realized what he wanted and couldn't help but smile. Nodding, I began to sing the lullaby for him. He was really too old for lullabies, but I was happy to do something to comfort him, considering the weight of my offenses.

He listened, staring gravely at the stars overhead, his fur drawn up to his chin.

He looked so like my boys Hun and Gavid that when he finally dozed, I couldn't help but stroke his dark curls back from his brow.

I waited for his sleep to deepen, and then I rose and went to hunt. As I did the night before, I brought food back to the camp for him, meat and some mushrooms I'd discovered growing on an outcrop of rocks. I slipped quietly beside him.

The fire was low and rosy. I watched the air ripple with the heat, the rhythmic way the embers glowed and dimmed inside the flames. Ilio turned over suddenly and squeezed up close to me, making me stiffen in alarm. But my belly was full of reindeer blood and my flesh was soft and warm with it. I felt no urge to drink his blood, as full as I was, and I suppose I felt like a normal man to him, at least for the moment.

It felt good to me. So good, in fact, I might have wept. It had been so long since I held my children in my arms. My mind crowded with memories, memories which were as sweet as they were heartbreaking. I put my arm over him. I held him close as he slept, thinking of the children I'd lost to time.

8

The featureless tundra seemed to stretch endlessly ahead of us, but we continued south at Ilio's insistence. Every now and then, the arid emptiness was broken by a line of low hills or a few trees gathered around a small creek or pool of water, but for the most part, the world was little more than two parallel planes: flat grasslands and empty blue sky.

On the third day, gray clouds crowded into the heavens, threatening rain—or snow, perhaps—but there was no precipitation, and the clouds finally drifted past.

Within three days, I had mastered the tongue of Ilio's people. Our language barrier broken, Ilio told me of the monster who'd killed his uncle—the frizzy headed hunter named Lene'Hab—and all the rest of his party. His recounting filled me with shame, but I was glad he seemed to have no suspicion that I was the monster he spoke of. He confirmed what I'd supposed earlier, that he was an orphan being raised by the hunters of his tribe. I agreed to accompany him the rest of the way to the base camp of the Mammoth Hunters, which was about five days further south.

His people called themselves the Denghoi, he told me, which basically meant the Mammoth People, although there had been fewer of the wooly beasts of late, and his people were beginning to rely more and more on the fish in the nearby lakes and streams, and the herds of reindeer that thundered across the tundra, for their livelihood.

"I guess when all the dengh are gone, we will have to call ourselves the Hap'phenoi. The Reindeer People," he said solemnly.

I chuckled sympathetically. "I suppose so."

"Where are your people from, Thest Un Mann?" he asked me.

I shrugged. "I do not know. Far away from here, I suppose. I was hurt and lost my way, and now I do not know how to get back to them."

"That's sad. Did you have children?"

"Yes. Many children."

"Did you love them?"

I frowned at the boy, who was walking stride by stride beside me. "Of course I did."

He nodded. "I'm sure my father loved me, too, although I don't really remember him. He was killed when I was a baby. A great bull ran him down and squashed him during a hunt. That is what my uncle told me. Dengh are very heavy, and the males will knock you down and step on you if they get angry. My mother died the year after. She got sick with the coughing illness and the medicine woman could not heal her."

"My mother died when I was young, too," I told him. "A venomous serpent struck her on the heel."

"Really?"

"Yes."

"I bet you missed her a lot."

"Yes, I did. I still do. I try to hold all the people I love in my heart. If you don't forget them, then they are not completely gone, even when they pass on to the afterlife."

Ilio nodded. "I think you're a very wise man," he said. "I'm glad I found you."

I nodded, feeling very ashamed of myself.

Rod Redux

Travelling with the boy was very agreeable to me. At night, after he'd fallen asleep, I stole away to hunt for us both. When I returned, I snuggled up to him and slept as a living man slept: at night, with the stars gleaming in the heavens over my head. As long as I filled my belly with blood every night, my thirst was not too difficult to resist, although I was a little fearful to let myself slumber beside him at first, afraid I might attack him in my sleep without knowing I was doing it. After a night or two, however, I put that fear to rest. My vampire body did not harm him of its own accord while my mind was dreaming.

Travelling in the daylight was uncomfortable. Vampire eyes are extremely sensitive. I can see in pitch dark as easily as a human sees in broad daylight, so you can imagine my misery traveling in the sunlit hours. Imagine staring into a stage light for twelve hours straight every day, and perhaps you will understand.

The morning of the sixth day I traveled with the boy, as I was lying asleep beside the fire, I felt warm living fingers exploring my flesh and roused in alarm.

Ilio was lying awake beside me, and he was stroking the skin of my shoulder and chest, where my clothing had gaped in my slumber. "Your skin is very strange. It is cold and smooth like stone," he said. He moved to touch my face and I rolled away from him, pushing his hand aside.

"My people are different than yours," I told him. Thinking fast, I expanded upon the lie, "My people are from an icy land with lots of snow, far to the north. That is why my skin is so pale and cold."

He nodded. "Your eyes are different, too. When it's dark, the firelight fills them up. It's very peculiar."

Ilio was a bright, curious boy. Had I thought he was oblivious to my vampiric traits? Ha! I was the oblivious one.

I was more careful to deceive him after that.

He noticed I never ate. It seemed to disturb him so I pretended to share meals with him. I would bring the food to my lips as if I was putting it in my mouth, but instead of putting it in my mouth, I would cup it in my palm and work my jaw like I was chewing. He also noticed that I did not need to empty my bladder or bowels. He asked me to accompany him to the bushes, and when I told him I did not need to go for the tenth time, he demanded, "Don't you ever need to pee or poop?" I shrugged, unsure how to explain that one. Finally, when he would not budge on it, I said, "My people don't do that very often. But you go ahead. I will guard you while you relieve yourself."

If he was older and more experienced, my strange habits might have alarmed him more, but he was still a year away from manhood, at least. He'd yet to get his first real spurt of growth, and his body was hairless aside from a bit of fuzz on his upper lip.

His youth was probably all that preserved my ruse. Children are so much easier to deceive. For them, the world is full of strange, unknowable things.

The days began to grow a little warmer as we travelled, the land more hilly and populous with trees and shrubbery and bodies of water.

"We're very near my home," he said, examining the landscape around us. He finally seemed at ease, happy almost. He no longer jumped at every strange noise. He no longer clung like a babe to me at night when we slept by the fire. Perhaps he thought we'd finally escaped the monster that had hunted his people, left it behind in the colder climes of the northern country. Perhaps our nearness to his home was comfort enough to ease his fears.

I found myself reluctant to part ways with the boy. I had grown fond of him. But I knew it was something I must do. I'd promised myself I would deliver him safe to the village of his people. If he stayed in my presence, I would eventually harm him, I knew, whether I wanted to or not. It was simply the nature of my curse.

Even as I loved him, I wanted to kill him and drink his blood.

I tried to push aside the urges, ignore the fantasies that flashed unbidden in my mind—holding him down, sinking my fangs into his throat, gulping the hot red blood that gushed out of him.

It would make me sad to part company with him, to be alone once again, but it was a necessary thing... for his sake.

At last we came upon a wooded rise. At the sight of it, the boy grew suddenly very excited. He looked at me with a broad grin, his blue eyes bright. "I know where we are now! The camp is just over this hill!" With that, he dashed ahead of me.

"Wait! Stay with me, Ilio!" I called, but he paid no heed.

Frowning, I jogged to catch up with him. I ascended the ridge and found him just on the other side of it, frozen in his tracks. He was staring down at the ruins of a small settlement. The blood had drained from his face. His mouth hung agape.

"What happened?" he asked softly, his eyes wide, uncomprehending.

I moved past him, scowling fiercely.

Down below, the village of the Denghoi lay in shambles. Human bodies sprawled in the dirt, unmoving. The huts and various wood structures of the village had been smashed flat or burned to the ground. There were no signs of life in the boy's semi-nomadic camp, not even a dog sniffing at the carcasses. The only movement in the destroyed camp was the fluttering clothes on the bodies of the dead, stirred by late winter's chill winds.

"What happened to everyone, Thest-un-Mann?" Ilio asked, trying to take my hand.

I pulled away from him. "Quiet, boy," I said. "Give me a

moment."

I opened my mind, allowing all the sensoria my vampiric senses could detect to come blasting into my awareness. One learns quickly, after the transformation, to block most of that sensory information out of the consciousness. It's that or be dazed by the sheer overwhelming copiousness of it—the miasma of smells and tastes, the overpowering stimulation of sight and sound and touch. You can let down your guard, let the whirlwind in, but first you must steel yourself for the assault. You must gather your strength to endure it.

As Ilio waited beside me, I opened my mind and let it all swirl in. The smells, the sounds, the tastes, the sights. The overriding impression was death, violence, panic. I was assaulted by the rank odor of dead human bodies, the acrid stench of charred wood and leather and woven plant textiles. I could smell the blood soaked into the earth, the phantom scent of fear hormones still lingering in the atmosphere, flyblown organs spilt from guts, the shit and piss that had dribbled from the bodies of the dying, now long dried.

Whatever tragedy befell the boy's people, it had occurred more than a week or two before our arrival. I sensed no marauders lingering in the woodlands that encircled the area. I sensed no living men for miles, aside from the boy at my side. The sun gleamed on the surface of the creek that wound alongside the settlement, and carrion birds swept through the air, turning in slow circles in the sky. Yet in the village, there was only death, long grown cold and bloated.

I turned to Ilio then and took his shoulders in my hands. "Now listen to me, boy. I want you to sit right here beside this bush while I walk down to your village to investigate. I don't want you to follow. Believe me, this is something you don't want to see up close."

His eyes glimmered moistly as he stared up at me. "But what happened? Why is everything burned? There are dead people down there, lying on the ground! I can see them."

"I know. Just stay here. I promise I'll be right back."

Ilio obeyed, sitting abruptly.

I turned then and descended the escarpment toward the camp.

As I approached, the smell of death and violence and blood and ash grew ever stronger, until finally my lips peeled back from my teeth and I had to hold my breath to keep from inhaling any more of it. The stew of foulness made my head spin, sickened me more than just physically.

I was sickened to my soul.

I walked through the remnants of the village, just charred sticks and cold coals now. The Denghoi employed mammoth tusks as part of the construction material of their homes. The ivory was charred, but not consumed, as the wood and hides had been. It gave the impression that their dwellings were not homes so much as great dead beasts, blackened and subsiding into the earth.

There were a multitude of tracks in the bare earth: humans, dogs, the little scavengers that came down from the forest to feast on the bodies, like raccoons and opossums, and there were bird tracks too, the markings of buzzards and crows. But there was another kind of track I'd never seen before, a crescent-shaped mark racing all through the village.

I traced the crescent impressions, trying to imagine what kind of beast would leave such a marking behind, but the sign was an enigma to me. I'd encountered no creature in the valley of the River People that could make such a footprint.

Finally, I turned to examine the bodies.

A female with long, braided hair lay stiff in the dirt a few strides away from me, her belly bloated with gas. Her neck was so mangled it was a wonder her head was still attached to her body. Her belly had been torn open and her entrails dragged out and partially eaten. Insects crawled among the bits of dirt and ash that adhered to her intestines.

A little further away was a young boy. He was lying on his face, his pale body naked and deeply lacerated. His sad little body displayed the markings of blunt injuries, and there was one of the crescent-shaped markings stamped into his spine, just above his buttocks.

Here, an old man clutched a knife in his cold fist, his frizzy white beard stained black with dried blood. There, another female, plump and fetching in life, perhaps, but dead and stiff now, her eyes empty sockets, her tongue protruding from her lips. Her throat was mangled as well, though not, I noted, as violently as the first's.

At the center of the devastation, several bodies were piled haphazardly, one atop the other. The injuries all the Denghoi people suffered were terribly familiar. Wounds to the neck.

Blood Drinkers! I thought to myself.

I was not frightened, but I was angry, and—dare I admit—mightily intrigued. In all my years, I had met no other Blood Drinkers like me, aside from the vicious pair who had plundered my own valley home so very long ago. Of course, I was thinking of the strange little vampire slave that moved like a lizard, and his master, the fiend who made me an immortal. And now, here was evidence of others like myself!

I stood, feeling a heady combination of excitement and apprehension, and I reached out with my senses again, hoping to catch some clue to the direction the Blood Drinkers had departed, hoping perhaps that I would find them at the furthest limits of my faculties, that they were not as long gone as it appeared they were.

Alas! I could detective no evidence of their presence.

But Ilio, I noticed, had chosen to disobey me. He weaved among the charred remains of his people's camp, his face white and drawn with shock even as his eyes jerked this was and that. I turned to chastise him, but saw that he had squatted and was pushing his fingers through the ash of a burned down hut. He pulled a charred figure from the rubble —a carving of a man. It was blackened and its crudely shaped legs had been broken off at the knees. He turned it in his hands, his eyes glittering with tears, then threw it down with an angry expression and walked swiftly toward me.

"Can we leave now, Thest-un-Mann?" he asked, choking only a little on his tears. "There's nothing left here for me. It is all gone, and everyone is dead. I'm the only Denghoi that lives now."

"Yes," I said sympathetically. I reached out and pulled him to my cold body. "I'm so sorry, Ilio. Let us leave this sad place."

The Country of the Ground Scratchers

1

Before we departed the village of the Denghoi, Ilio and I gathered together what few valuables lay strewn in the ruins, items left behind by the marauders which the fires had not destroyed. The boy was anxious to leave, but I knew we would need the supplies. There were several things lying in the rubble that would be useful in the days ahead.

We recovered a few knives and a hatchet made of stone. I also found some bone needles and eating utensils in the remains of one hut, and a couple intact spears. We put the small things we collected in our clothes pouches and, carrying the larger items in our hands, moved on.

Ilio, I noticed, had retrieved the broken figure he'd unearthed earlier. He secreted it in his pocket without comment, trying to keep me from seeing him do it by turning his back to me.

Instead of continuing south, as we would be forced to cross the river, I suggested we head east, toward the wooded ridge that rose up from the destroyed village. I'd grown up in a densely forested river valley, and knew I would feel more comfortable traveling through the woodlands. I had no love for the wide open plains of the steppe, and the foliage would help shield the boy from the cold winds that swept the region.

Ilio shrugged. "It doesn't matter which way we go," he said. "Not anymore."

He said this in an emotionless way that pained me, his eyes distant and mournful. I wanted to say something to comfort him, but was there anything I could possibly say that would mitigate his loss? His whole world had been stripped away from him.

And I, unbeknownst to the boy, had played no small part in this.

So I said nothing. I put my hand on his shoulder and drew him to me, and we walked east, away from his tribe's devastated camp.

As twilight approached, I built a big campfire in a clearing on the ridge, well out of sight of the plundered settlement. I made the fire near a burbling stream and Ilio went to it and drank, then sat beside the water for a while with his back to me. I tended the fire, poking it with a stick every now and then, and pretended I did not hear the boy's quiet tears. He'd taken the carving from his pocket and wept as he squeezed it in his hands.

We had a little meat left from the day before, and I foraged some edible shoots and roots on the slopes around us. My wives, I'm sure, could have collected a tastier assortment of plants, but I was pretty confident none of my selections would poison the boy. When Ilio finally sought my company, his cheeks scrubbed dry, I passed him some food and he ate.

"My people believe a spirit dwells within all things," I said casually, pretending to chew. "Me, you, that tree, this stone. It is our belief that when a thing from this world dies or is destroyed, the essence within it lives on. For some things, like a stone or a tree, the spirit returns to the earth and is reborn, but the essence of living things, it is said by my people, their spirits ascend into the heavens, where they reside for all time, watching down over us." I gestured up at the sky, in which there twinkled a multitude of faint stars.

Ilio looked up at the stars thoughtfully.

"Do you think that's true?" he asked finally.

"Why not?" I shrugged. "Even if it's not true, it's a soothing thought."

Ilio's eyes cut sharply toward me, then he smiled. "You're not very good at consoling people," he said.

I laughed. "It's not one of my strengths."

We talked for a while after that.

Ilio told me of his peoples' spiritual beliefs, which were polytheistic and sounded quite complex, lots of gods and goddesses with complicated relationships and very human foibles. Very similar to recent Nordic beliefs—recent to me, that is; rather ancient to you modern readers. It sounded as if it was all very entertaining to listen to on long winter nights, I suppose, but I was not converted.

He talked about his uncle and the other Mammoth Hunters who'd taken care of him when his mother died and no one else in the village was willing to look after him. His uncle had been a rough-edged fellow, but had made sure Ilio was fed and clothed. The old man Elk had been his grandfather's brother, the eldest in their tribe. He told me of them all, and I suffered for every one.

I told him about my wives and children, the peaceful valley where I was born, and the big, gentle Neanderthals who were our neighbors. He seemed very interested when I told him about my children, and laughed out loud several times when I described some of their more amusing antics.

It was growing late by then. I could see his eyes getting heavy, and he yawned several times as we conversed. I finally told him it was time for sleep, and he did not object. I watched him unfold his outer coat into a sleeping bag—wondering again at the clever way his people had made them-- and I poked at the fire while he wiggled in and settled down for the night.

He pulled his cover over his head and went to sleep quickly. When soft snores issued from the lump across the fire from me, I rose silently to my feet and slipped away from the light of the campfire.

At the edge of the clearing, I disrobed so that I did not get blood on my garments or snag them on the branches of the trees, and then I flew up into the boughs.

I flashed through the treetops, hunting for something hot and full of blood. Ilio's constant nearness taxed my restraint. All through the evening, the smell of his blood made the dark hunger roil and snap inside me. I could feel my veins contracting, my skin shriveling. I needed to feed.

I leapt from branch to branch, enjoying my freedom. My flight through the forest was exhilarating, a thing I'd enjoyed since my days looking after the River People when it was the only joy I had left to me, my lust for blood so overpowering I dared not venture near my loved ones.

I snatched a fat raccoon from its burrow in a hollow log. An owl met its doom at my fangs. I rustled through the forest canopy like a swift, dark wind.

Further on, I spied a deer on the ground below, bedded for the night in a tangle of thorn bushes, and I dropped down on it from above to tear its neck open. It made a bleating cry and struggled beneath me as I fed on its blood, but I only held it tighter and drew its life into my mouth more forcefully. When it finally went limp in my arms and my belly was tight as a drum, I threw it over my shoulders and hiked back to our campsite.

Ilio still slept.

I hung the carcass in a tree a little distance away to keep the scavengers from it. The deer's struggles, and the journey back to camp, had splattered me with its blood. Instead of dressing, I walked naked to the brook to bathe. Squatting down by the water, I scrubbed my face and arms and chest, washing all the dried blood off me. My cold flesh gleamed, white and steaming, in the starlight.

Ilio stirred when I approached the fire to dry myself. His eyes cracked open and he smiled faintly, then the whites showed and he began to snore again.

I dressed, then retrieved a dry hunk of kindling and one of the stone knives we'd recovered from the Denghoi rubble. I sat cross-legged by the fire. As Ilio slept, I began to whittle a shape in the timber. I worked at my carving for several hours, employing a bit of my vampiric speed to shave the surface of the log away rapidly. The knife was a blur in my white hands. Curlicues and bits of wood drifted down upon my thighs.

As I carved a plaything for the boy, I recalled the long ago nights I sat in my own home by the fire and carved trifles for my sleeping children. The memory filled me with melancholy, but when I was finished with the carving, that melancholy turned to pride and anticipation. I'd carved a very realistic likeness of a Mammoth Hunter for the young orphan, and I couldn't wait to give it to him when he awoke.

"I found something for you," I told him in the morning when he rose, yawning, from his bedding.

"What is it?" he asked.

I swung the wooden carving from behind me and passed it to him with a grin.

I watched his eyes light up. He looked at me with a wondrous smile and in that instant, I knew I loved him completely.

He turned the carving in his hands, smiling and wiping his eyes, then jumped into my arms and hugged me. "Thank you, Thest. Thank you!" And though he tried to hide it from me—I suppose he thought he was too old for such things—I caught him several times, playing with the wooden hunter by the brook, making low noises as the little figure battled imaginary enemies. I even overhead him speaking for the plaything in a low and murmuring voice.

I never allowed myself to forget my offenses against the child, but I pushed my guilt and shame aside so that I could love him selflessly, nurture him without reservation. In the months that followed, I cared for him as if he was my own son, and I watched him grow and mature with the pride of a father.

Oh, Ilio--! My first vampire child... How I sinned against you--!

I loved you, even as you struck me down.

I begged you to forgive me, even in the face of your hatred.

If only I could go back and change the things I did.

2

We travelled in a southeasterly direction, moving through the low forested hills as the trees budded and spring came round to the continent of Europe.

As the weather grew warmer, Ilio took to wearing just a loincloth. I could see him maturing day by day, and it filled me with a mixture of sorrow and admiration. By the end of summer, he had grown at least four inches, and was transforming into a slim and muscular young man. His body rippled powerfully when he ran through the forest. His face began to take on the contours of the man he would become. By the time autumn came around, his thick black hair had grown down past his shoulders, and he began braiding it so that it swung about his face and shoulders in coils. Soon, he would be grown, and he would leave me to start a family of his own, I knew, so I took a secret delight when I caught him playing with the little wooden men and animals that I'd added to his collection, when the mood seized me to carve them.

It seemed that winter came in the blink of an eye. We settled in a cave in a mountainous region bordering the Pannonian Plain, in the country that is now called Austria, and it was there I spent my days teaching the boy the skills he would require to survive on his own.

I taught him to flake stone so he could make his own knives and arrowheads and chopping instruments. I taught him how to construct a bow, how to tan hides, how to cut and sew clothing. Ilio was a bright boy. A quick study, you would say in these modern times. He even improved on the snares and weaving skills I imparted to him.

I no longer tried to hide from him the peculiar quality of my skin. He loved me as I loved him and had grown accustomed to my strange appearance. He even joked about it from time to time. "You're as pale as a frog's belly!" he teased me one afternoon, as we bathed together in the pool beside our home.

Winter had passed, a mild season of cold, and spring had returned to the Alps once again. It was the first truly warm day of the season, and we'd dashed for the falls to swim, even though it was still cold enough to make us both yelp when we jumped in.

I twisted my hair to wring out the water. "You'd probably be a couple shades lighter if you washed more often," I retorted, teasing him in return.

Ilio laughed. "I like being dirty. The stronger I smell, the better I like it."

"That's not a good thing if you ever want wives. Women don't want a husband who smells like a skunk."

Paddling about in the pool, Ilio said, "Tell me about your wives again, Thest."

So I told him about Eyya and Nyala, what they'd looked like, how I'd won their favor. He listened with keen interest, then wanted to know what it felt like to mate with a woman, and more importantly, how exactly it was done.

His question caught me off guard, and I looked at him with my mouth open for a moment, too flabbergasted to answer him. I realized then, gaping at the boy, that he'd blossomed like the forest around us had blossomed. He was growing sideburns. There were wispy patches of hair on his chin and upper lip. There was no hair on his penis yet, but I noted it was bigger than it was before. My little Ilio was growing up.

Of course, you know if you read the first volume of my memoirs that I grew up in a very open society, sexually. The River People were ancestor worshippers, our culture based on group families and fertility rituals. We revered sex and celebrated it as the wellspring of our continuation. We didn't regard it with shame, or believe that it was the root of all evil in the world, as the modern Christians aver. In my culture, community orgies, psychotropic drug use and homosexual bonding rituals were the norms. It didn't embarrass me to explain the mechanics of sex to the boy, or admit to him how pleasurable the act was. I was only shocked by his sudden interest in it, how I'd failed to realize he was no longer a boy, and would be feeling his first stirrings of sexual desire.

"Have you never seen your uncle or any of the other men in your village engage in sex?" I asked.

Ilio shook his head. "No. They always put up curtains when they lay down with their women. At least, my uncle did. He said it was man's weakness that he must return to the womb, and that we should hide that weakness from view, lest others make a mockery of it."

I shook my head. "My people were not ashamed of their pleasures. It is the act that makes children… and keeps our wives tolerant of us. Why be embarrassed of it?"

"I'm not ashamed," Ilio said. Then he finally confided,

"When I was cleaning my penis yesterday, it grew rigid and then a sticky fluid squirted out of it. It never did that before. It felt really good. Does your penis do that, Thest?"

I laughed. "So that is what this sudden curiosity is all about!" Sobering, I replied, "That's a perfectly natural thing, and, yes, that is what happens to mine if I... *ahem!* clean it too rigorously. Don't worry about it, boy. That is merely your body pouring forth its seed, and when you take a wife and you impart your seed within her belly, it will grow into a baby inside her."

Ilio nodded, relieved. "I just hope mine grows as large as yours."

"It may grow even larger," I conceded. "When it comes to that, the size of the branch varies with the tree."

It was a time I think back on fondly now, the raising of the child Ilio. I'd lost my own family when I was made into a vampire. In those first few decades of my vampiric existence, I was barely able to control my bloodlust, if at all, and could only watch my children grow from afar. I did not dare come near them, lest I bring them to harm. With Ilio, I was a much older Blood Drinker. I had more control of my hunger. I could enjoy the rearing of a child, for I considered him a son no less than the sons of my own flesh-- Gan and Hun, Gavid and Den. That's not to say I didn't hunger for his blood. In fact, my craving for his blood drove me to hunt the forest nightly, gorging on the blood of any unfortunate animal that crossed my path. My wicked appetite was bearable only when I was glutted on the blood of the forest wildlife, my belly straining with it.

Ilio was a good son. He overlooked my faults. He was respectful of my decisions, mindful of his chores and took great pleasure in my approval. He strutted when I complimented his skills with a bow. He beamed when I exclaimed over the size of a deer he'd killed, or the cleverness of his snares.

Over time, he noticed further peculiarities about my vampire nature. Once, when I laughed out loud at his wit, he took note of my fangs. He later asked if all my people had fangs like a wolf, and I answered, "Yes, Ilio."

When I asked if my teeth frightened him, he shrugged and said, "No more than anything else about you. We are just made differently, I suppose."

Finally, one rainy afternoon, he demanded to know why I left the cave at night, when I thought he was sleeping. He wanted to know where I was going, what I was doing.

"I am hunting, Ilio," I answered. "I do not eat food as you do. When you were younger, I pretended to eat so you wouldn't be frightened of me, but you are older now. You know that I love you, and I wish to be honest with you. I hunt at night when you are sleeping. I catch my prey and suck the blood from their bodies. I have an illness and that is how I must eat."

Ilio shuddered. "That's disgusting."

I nodded. "Yes. It is."

But later that night, as I waited for him to grow sleepy, he smiled at me affectionately and said, "You can go hunting, Thest. You do not need to wait until I sleep."

Returning his smile, I rose and unlaced my boots and breeches. "So I do not tear them, or stain them with blood," I explained, stepping out of them. I crossed the cave to the opening, naked, then looked back at him and said, "I will return shortly."

"Be careful," he called to me as he sat by the fire. He was stringing his bow.

"I promise," I chuckled, then flew into the night.

Sometimes, during my nightly hunts, I ranged further out than was necessary. I climbed to the highest tree I came across and I gazed out across the darkened landscape. To the east across the endless plains, to the mountains in the west, I reached out with my vampire senses, searching for others of my kind. I had not forgotten the evidence of their predations, the plundered village of the Denghoi, so I maintained a vigil, both for Ilio's safety and my own curiosity.

I searched the ground sometimes for more of those strange, crescent tracks, but I never found anything of note, no vampires, no strange beasts with moon-shaped footprints. I spotted human nomads sometimes, travelling in small groups across the grassy plains or picking their way through rocky passes in the mountains, but no other vampires like me. Still, I searched, and I often wondered what my vampire brethren looked like, how they behaved, what deities they might believe in or myths they might extoll.

The only vampires I'd ever seen were the fiends who'd accosted the peaceful valley where I'd been born: the strange little blood-drinker and his powerful, vile master-- the creature who stole away my life.

Another summer passed, then autumn and winter. It grew bitter cold. We hung hides across the entrance of our cave and huddled around the fire. Winter made Ilio surly. He was restless and cranky. My little boy was just a head shorter than I now. His face was pebbly with acne, his mustache growing in. I think he spent half the cold season sleeping and the other half masturbating. He was so hormonal the cave stank of his burgeoning manhood. Finally, when spring came round again, he asked if we could leave our home in the mountains.

"I want to travel again, Thest," he said, his voice husky, having deepened in the past three months. "I want to be around other people. I want to find a woman to lie with."

I nodded. Of course. I knew he'd fly the nest someday. This was as it should be. It should come as no surprise to me. "Where do you want to go?" I asked him, my heart breaking just a little at the thought.

"South," he answered eagerly. Did he think I would object? I only ever thought of what was best for him. "My uncle used to talk of a tribe called the Oombai," he said, "Though he usually called them the Ground Scratchers. They used to trade with the Denghoi before my people were all killed. He said they were an odd tribe, and that they worship some strange goddess who lives beneath the earth, but the women of their country are plentiful and very fair to look at. So he said."

I clapped him on the shoulder. "Then South it is, Ilio."

3

It saddened me to think of leaving our little burrow in the mountains. There were so many things I knew I'd miss. I'd miss its grand view of the Pannonian Plain, the sight of the endless grasslands shining under the moon, so still and calm and peaceful. I'd miss the forest and the falls. I'd miss my nightly hunting excursions, the abundant wildlife, the simplicity of the life we'd made together, all alone here on this mountain, but Ilio was becoming a man, and I knew it was time for him to seek out others of his kind. I'd possessed him long enough.

It was time to find a new home for him.

We gathered what belongings we could comfortably carry and said good-bye to our cozy little warren. As Ilio bent to his preparations, I surveyed our home for the last time: the plush furs we'd covered the floor with, and all the boy's wall paintings. Ilio had covered the walls with handprints and paintings of deer and fish. He'd even made a drawing of me, a white humanoid figure with two orange dots for eyes. I was not too keen of his paintings at first. My people were superstitious of such things, but I grew accustomed to them eventually. Even came to appreciate their beauty. I would miss our home.

"Are you ready to go?" I asked him, placing my torch against a rock near the entrance. Its flames whipped and made a sputtering sound in the wind that swirled through the mouth of the cavern.

Ilio tied off his pack and sat back with a sigh. He looked all around the cave, his eyes large and grave, and I watched his brow furrow with emotion. I was glad to see the hesitation on his face. I felt less maudlin, then.

"This was a good home," he said.

"Yes, it was."

I made a point not to look back as we departed.

We picked our way down the familiar footpaths toward the grassy plains, the moon high and bright, the late spring breeze balmy and pleasant. Ilio walked ahead of me, excited to be underway.

"Do you think we'll ever come back here?" he asked as we descended the rocky scree, sliding a little in the loose soil.

"No," I answered.

I was tempted to reach out and snag him, lest he turn his ankle. Young men are so careless!

"Oh." He ducked his head and dropped back beside me, lost in his thoughts for a good distance. The mountain slope had leveled out. Our legs swished through knee-high grass. "I'll miss our home," he said finally.

"As will I," I replied, and I put my hand on his shoulder.

The country of the Ground Scratchers was many days travel across the southern plains, but the dry sea basin was flat, and the grass, so early in the year, was rarely higher than our hips. We were lucky. The weather was mild and game was abundant. We only had difficulty once, and it was my fault.

Four days journey from the cave where we'd stayed so long, I ranged out further than I ever had during my nightly hunts. The moon was fat and bright, and I had detected a strange scent on the wind, a thing I'd never smelled before. I followed the strange scent out into the plains, roaming so far from our camp I could no longer see the light of its fire or sense my young companion sleeping next to it.

Without Ilio's limitations to accommodate, I could take to the winds, which was a pleasure to me.

Vampires cannot actually fly, just so you know. We can leap great distances. We can move at such speeds that we skate through the air, guiding our movements with our bodies. The trillions of tiny cells that compose our physical form, you see, are hollow chambers. We are not sloshing bags of water, like you humans. Though we are very resilient, we are mostly empty things, granular masses of lifeless, dried up cell capsules. You'd be surprised how little we actually weigh, and it's that emptiness, like the hollow bones of a bird, or dry cork, which allows us to glide through the air, an outlandish trick, to be sure, but quite exhilarating.

But I digress.

On a wooded hill, I found the black scorch mark of a months-old campfire. There were several faded footprints on the ground around the coals, the markings of leather-clad feet and canines, and near the trees, the same crescent markings I'd encountered in the desolated village of the Denghoi, the moon-shaped imprints of an unfamiliar beast-- heavy things, I could tell, because the impressions were deeper than the others. It was the first signs I'd encountered of the mysterious Others in more than a year!

The camp was long abandoned, but their smell and the smell of their beasts lingered, albeit faintly.

Sometime the previous autumn, my vampire brethren had passed within a few days journey of our home. So close, and yet I had failed to sense them! Touching the faded markings in the earth, I inhaled their ghostly scents and fixed them in my memory.

The discovery was terribly exciting for me. I wanted to meet these other vampires. I wanted to lay eyes on other beings like myself.

They could be brutal, I knew. These Others had devastated Ilio's people, but was I any less vicious? In my hunger, I could be just as cruel.

I decided I would seek them out, once I'd found a suitable home for my adopted human child, and thinking that, I rose and resumed my hunt for blood.

I was tracking a wild boar through the grassland when I heard, very weak with distance, a frightened cry arise in the moonlight.

Ilio--!

I heard him call my name, his voice gone shrill with fear. It echoed across the open plains. *"The-eeeeeest!"*

For half a second, I froze where I was standing, paralyzed by the terror in the young man's voice, then I turned on my heel and bolted across the undulating plain. I shot across the grassy prairie, fear transforming my heart to ice. I cut through the savanna with such speed that the hip-high grass parted behind me in a widening V, hissing like the surface of the sea in the wake of a fast boat.

As I arrowed through the plains, my feet barely touching the ground, my ears picked up snatches of a confrontation: crude demands and low, cruel laughter. I heard Ilio's grunts and cries of pain, and caught the smell of strange, filthy men.

There--! Now I could see them! They were still small with distance but drawing rapidly nearer by the second.

Two nomads had stumbled across our camp and were accosting the boy. I could see the interlopers in the firelight. Burly men with spears and long tangled hair, their faces painted red and black.

My adopted son was struggling with the smaller of the two marauders while the bigger one was lowering his leggings

Rod Redux

in preparation of sodomizing the young man.

Ilio kicked his legs and yelled in protest. They'd already peeled off his breeches.

Laughing, the smaller man wrestled the boy to submission.

As I swept through the campsite like a hurricane wind, whistling past the struggling trio, I threw out my right hand and let it collide with the back of the smaller bandit's head. My fist struck his skull with enough force to tear his head clear off his neck. Blood and brains sprayed in the air, splattering my arm and chest and face. The brigand's pulped head went spinning off into the grassland. Where it landed, I knew not... nor did I really care.

The impact fissured the flawless white flesh of my right hand. As I skidded to a stop and turned to launch myself at the bigger man, the Living Blood inside me healed the webbing of cracks almost instantly. Before the smaller man's decapitated head even hit the ground, my hand was whole again.

The headless man was still holding Ilio's wrists. His body hadn't realized its top was missing yet.

With a snarl, I flew toward the bandit trying to assault my child. I hooked my fingers into his tunic and lifted him from the ground, his leggings tangled round his ankles. We sailed twenty feet past the campsite before returning to the earth and went rolling in the grass. I came up overtop him and loosed a ferocious hiss, letting him get a good look at my blazing eyes and wolf-like fangs, then my jaws lunged down into the unwashed meat of his neck and I tore his pudgy flesh open.

He screamed as I ripped and gnawed into him. He caught my hair and tried to pull my fangs from his throat, but it was too late. He was dead already. He just didn't know it yet.

In my outrage and fury, I was wanton. I drained him dry, ripping and mauling his body in the process. I always lose control of myself when I feed, but when I kill in anger, I'm a raging demon.

When I was done with him, he lay in pieces, and I was soaked in his blood.

I sat back, blinking in horror at the mess I had made. My body was covered in blood and flesh and slivers of shivering organ meat.

"Thest?" Ilio murmured, approaching me cautiously.

"Stay back, Ilio!" I commanded gruffly. "Don't come near me!"

I felt him stiffen in fear, then said more gently. "Please, boy. Go back to the fire."

I sensed him withdraw and tried to get a grip on my blood-hunger. For a second, I'd almost lunged at him. I took a deep breath and wrestled the ravening demon in me. I felt the hunger abate. It coiled up inside me, grudgingly, grumbling in complaint. I surveyed the mess beneath me with distaste, then rose from the mound of torn meat and slippery entrails.

I looked at my hands. Gore dripped and dribbled from my cold white fingers. I felt the sticky fluids trickle down my beard and chest and legs.

"Close your eyes, Ilio," I implored when I returned to the fire. "I don't want you to look at me."

"Thest—" he started to protest.

"Please, Ilio. I ask this for me. Not for you."

"Yes, Thest."

When I saw that he had closed his eyes, I stepped into the firelight and seized the body of the smaller bandit. I grasped it by the ankle and dragged the corpse away into the grass. I carried the flopping cadaver to the carnage of its companion and heaped it onto the deconstructed remains, then walked away to find a pool to bathe in.

It was a good thing I'd disrobed to hunt that night, as was my habit. If not, my clothing would have been ruined by all the blood.

Rod Redux

The pool was marshy and surrounded by reeds, but it was deep and refreshing, and I walked into it until the water came up to my chest. I stood for a moment, looking at the gelid reflection of the moon on the surface of the pond. Wisps of fog rose from the tiny, rippling mere, drifting in pale tendrils in the chill night air.

How many times have I washed the blood of murdered men from this cold white body? I wondered. That was a question I could not answer. Countless times, for sure, and I did it one more time that night-- washed the blood of murdered men from my skin-- feeling sullied and morose, before I returned to check on Ilio.

"Are you hurt?" I asked, stepping into the firelight.

Ilio was sitting near the fire, swaddled in his bedding. He jumped a little at my question, turned his head to look at me. "I am uninjured," he answered, relieved to see me. "They said they wanted our belongings, then the smaller one tried to hold me down and so his big companion could mate with me."

"I know. I'm sorry. I was far away and didn't know there were others nearby. I was careless."

"It's not your fault, Thest. You saved me." He looked away, his bulging blue eyes turned toward the dark horizon, his face troubled, as it often seemed troubled, with too many thoughts. I was struck once again by his resemblance to my old companion Brulde. That same pensive stare. "I tried to fight them off, but I was not strong enough."

"You are still growing," I said, drawing near the fire so that its warmth could dry my skin. "You'll be big enough to protect yourself soon. Don't be ashamed. I've been bested in combat myself, when I was still a..." I let my words trail off.

"Man?" Ilio suggested.

"Yes," I said softly.

"You were a man like me once, weren't you, Thest?" Ilio asked, his eyes turning to my face suddenly.

"I'm a man still. You see the evidence hanging here," I said, trying to make the boy laugh.

Ilio smiled wanly. "You know what I mean."

I sighed. I picked up my clothing and began to dress myself. "Yes. I was a man like you once. My skin was ruddy. I had no fangs. I was soft and warm and alive."

"So what happened to you?" Ilio asked. His eyes bored into me. His look made me anxious. How could one so young look so deeply into another's heart?

I sat cross-legged near the fire with him. "I will tell you that story, Ilio. I promise. But not tonight. It unsettles me to kill. It's not in my nature to be violent."

Ilio smiled sympathetically. "I understand." He scooted beside me and put his head on my shoulder. After a moment or two, he raised his head up and squinted at me. "Your flesh is warm."

I nodded. With a bitter smile, I said, "Yes… but only for a little while."

4

After that, our journey continued without incident, and we came at last into the country of the Ground Scratchers.

Very soon after entering their territory, I had to agree with Ilio's uncle. The Ground Scratchers were a strange people. The homes we passed were odd-shaped huts made of timber and thatch. They were much larger than the dome-shaped tents I'd lived in as a man, with peaked roofs and waist-high openings in the walls through which their occupants could peer outside. Some of the openings were decorated with beaded hangings or weaves, which the humans had to push aside if they wanted to look out. These thatched huts looked very sophisticated to me. I was impressed by the ingenuity their complex construction represented. Humanity had made great advances during my long sleep in the ice!

Surrounding the dwellings were broad yards studded with conical wooden structures. The wooden stakes were angled toward a common center and lashed together with twine, with vines twisted all around and through them. Strange green vegetables bobbed from the stems of the plants.

In the bare dirt yards between these strange vegetable cages, haggard men and women with short-cropped hair clawed at the earth with long wooden tools. Stone blades were lashed onto the ends of the handles, and they tirelessly thrust these triangular shaped blades into the ground and raked the crumbly soil back toward their feet.

We observed the humans working from a little distance, puzzled by their behavior. Whatever task they were set upon, it must have been quite important, for they worked without ceasing, and all the while, other humans in brightly colored garments watched over them, doing nothing but occasionally barking an order or slashing the bent back of one of the laborers with a switch.

"See how they scratch at the ground?" Ilio whispered to me. "It's like my uncle said."

"Very peculiar," I replied. "Why are they scratching the dirt like that?"

Ilio shrugged. "They worship a goddess who lives in the earth. I guess they're scratching her back."

I snorted. "Why? Does she have fleas?"

A few of the laborers took notice of our presence and stopped to ogle us, but they returned to their duties without accosting us, bending quickly to their work when their overseer barked at them.

The presence of so many humans gave me pause, but I sensed no malice in their glances. They seemed only tired and resigned. They smelled of sweat and dirt and a palpable sense of fatalism.

The stern men supervising their labor, on the other hand, pretended not to notice us.

We moved on, making our way up a steep hill. We were in no hurry, just wandering in a lackadaisical manner, taking in the sights like any other tourists would, regardless of the era. We were following a well-worn path that meandered in between the strange, peaked houses and the bare dirt yards where the laborers so diligently toiled. Here and there, men and women tended to fruit trees, and on a distant hillside, a group of humans labored in a field of flax, plucking some part of the stalk and stuffing it in their baskets. Flax, I knew, could be woven into string or the sophisticated textiles the people of this region seemed to favor. My people had used it to weave the string we sometimes used to sew our clothing together, though we'd never harvested it on such a scale.

The sun overhead was bright and warm. It stung my eyes like an infuriated scorpion, but I endured the discomfort for Ilio's sake. His head was swiveling tirelessly back and forth as he absorbed this country's outlandish sights: the strange homes with their bright decorations, the odd behavior of the inhabitants, the colorful beaded clothes of the labor masters.

As we rounded the hill, we could not help but falter in our tracks. Were we already impressed? Down below, stretching across a wide and sparsely wooded plain, all the way to the banks of a gleaming, serpentine river, was a village crowded with an uncountable number of dwellings. I'd never seen a settlement so large, or with so many huts! Judging by the expression on Ilio's face, he hadn't either. Men, women and children swarmed like ants through the avenues. Some of the lodges were truly massive-- by my primitive reckoning, anyway. There were extensive fields where groups of Ground Scratchers labored, hundreds of them it seemed, their bare backs bent to their duties. In other lots, fruit trees marched rank and file, rows upon rows of them. There was a large circular plaza in the center of the settlement, and herds of animals massed in wood enclosures.

"Shall we retreat?" I asked in a low voice, only half-joking.

Ilio looked at me apprehensively. "N-no. Let's go down there."

I glanced at him and nodded.

Hitching our packs, we descended.

As we passed through the village of the Ground Scratchers, my head began to spin. A whirlwind of inexplicable sights and sounds and smells bombarded my senses. Men and women dug ceaselessly at the bare dirt, or stood on their knees at the bases of large, food-bearing plants, picking at the leaves. Other humans dressed in brilliantly dyed garments stopped to gape at us as we passed them in the thoroughfares. Some of them were bedecked in preposterously ornate headgear, pendulous jewelry swinging from their earlobes or nipples or genitals. The women wore beaded skirts and collars of woven plant material cinched around their breasts, which made their teats stick out straight in front of them. The men wore cloaks with feathered collars and plaited vests. Some of them sported long, cylindrical gourds on their cocks, lashed round their hips with strings. The smell of feces was overwhelming. Rivulets of animal and human excrement ran along shallow troughs, or collected into hideous smelling pools in the low-lying areas of the settlement. We paused to listen to a trio of men playing musical instruments in an alley. The tune was loud and cheery. At the fore of the performers, a monkey on a leash turned flips and beat a tiny drum with a stick. We passed a construction of hewn timber that housed a herd of jostling reindeer, and then another enclosing great feathered beasts. The massive birds strutted upon powerful, bright orange legs as long as the boy was tall, their beaked heads rising up twice our height.

Ilio approached the enclosure, grinning up at one of the mighty raptors. I think he intended to pet it. The animal cocked an eye at him, spared him a withering glare, then promptly ducked its head and snatched a beak full of his hair.

"Owww!" he exclaimed, dodging back and rubbing his skull.

"Careful, boy," I laughed.

The presence of so many humans strained my composure. The smell of their warm-blooded bodies had whetted my appetite. I found myself wrestling with my blood-thirst before we'd even passed halfway through the encampment. There were so many of them, and they smelled so delicious! If I had not honed my self-control living with Ilio so many seasons, I might have run amok.

Yet, for all the village's glamor, there was a great disparity among its citizens, one which I did not look upon favorably. Some of the people who lived here were dressed in brightly dyed clothing. They wore great feathered headdresses or jeweled bands wrapped around their brows. Their faces were garishly decorated in livid hues of yellow and red and blue. They were well fed and their faces were untroubled. Yet the majority, the ones who labored in the soil, was naked or dressed in filthy rags. Their bent backs were striped with the scars of many a lash, and they seemed all to be half-starved, their ribs showing through their flesh, their joints knuckled. It was an appalling sight. To see so many men and women so starved, and in such an abundant land--! The disparity was quite distasteful to me, outrageous even, but being a foreigner, I felt I had little right to pass judgment on their society. How could I be so presumptuous? I wanted to suck the blood of every person who passed me by.

I expected to be challenged by the warriors who patrolled the avenues. There were quite a few of them, lean men with cruel, suspicious eyes, and all of them were well armed. They wore bone plated armor vests and shoulder pieces and helmets made of shell and woven plant material, with boar tusks or small antlers curving out from the sides. None challenged our presence, although a couple of them stopped to stare at us a moment before turning and racing away.

"They're running to tell their chieftain about us," I murmured to Ilio. "Are you sure these people are friendly to outsiders?"

Ilio looked at me apprehensively.

Before much time had passed, a procession of men rounded the corner and marched toward us. There were five wizened elders in the group, flanked on each side by a pair of armed guards. I came to a stop when I saw them and casually pushed Ilio behind me.

They approached until they were but six strides away, then the old men bowed to me, more or less in unison.

I bowed back, relieved that we were not immediately accosted.

The expressions on their faces were pleasant enough, and yet there was something about the old chieftains I was immediately suspicious of. I couldn't put my finger on it, not even with my enhanced senses, but they put my wind up, and I was careful of them from the outset.

Something in the aroma of their bodies struck me as peculiar. They looked like any other old men, smelled like any other old men, too: odor of sour sweat and shit. Yet there was an odd undertone to their scent that was not quite natural. It was faintly familiar, but what was it?

And it was not just their smell. The skin of the elders was the color of mahogany, deeply lined by years of exposure to the elements, but their flesh had a glossy texture that was just slightly unnatural. They moved strangely, too. Their backs were bent with age, but they moved their bodies with an ease that belied their advanced years. Their hair was frizzy and gray, but it was glossy as with youth, and their eyes were very bright and clear, not yellow and bloodshot and faded, as the eyes of old men naturally become as they wind their final years toward death.

They wore their authority in bright hues and jeweled adornments. Each was dressed in very elaborate woven garments—bright plated skirts, beaded shoulder mantles and headdresses-- and their faces were painted a pale green hue with swathes of black across the eyes, making the whites of their eyes seem even more unnatural.

We stood appraising one another, the air between our groups thick with tension, until finally one of the old men stepped forward and spoke.

The old man who stepped forward had a large nose, sunken cheeks and only two teeth in his mouth, one at each corner of his lips. The others seemed to slouch a little when he moved to address us. He must be their leader then, I thought.

"Weh owwhen-ah, potashu t'sukuru," he said.

Of course his language was foreign to me, but some of the words sounded like Denghoi words. *Owwhen-ah* sounded like the Denghoi word for "welcome" and *potashu* was very similar to the Denghoi word for "drink" or "water". It was not surprising their language was analogous to the tongue of the Mammoth Hunters, as the two cultures were located very near to one another geographically, and, according to Ilio, they had traded in the past. Nevertheless, even with my vampire knack for dialects, it would take me days to master their tongue, and I was stumped trying to decide how I should proceed with this confrontation.

Behind me, Ilio piped, "Do you speak Denghoi?"

The old man leaned to one side and peeked at my young companion, then said, "Yes, I speak Denghoi, though it has been many seasons since we traded with the Mammoth Hunters of the north."

"The Denghoi are no more. I am the last one," Ilio said.

I nudged the boy to silence him, said, "I am Thest. This is my companion Ilio."

The old man stood straight—as straight as his curved spine would allow-- and squinted up at me while scratching the hairy round paunch that hung over his plated skirt. "I am Bhulloch, Thest. I am the Chief Elder of the Oombai people. I speak the tongue of your kind, too, though I've never known a Blood Drinker to approach the village of the Oombai in the daylight. Your people always come with the twilight, from the mountains in the east." The old man's eyes narrowed slyly. "Are you an outcast?"

I did not like the old man's wily expression, so I cobbled up a quick lie. "I am a messenger. I've been sent on a long journey and sought a place to rest."

"And your… slave? I've never known a Blood Drinker who traveled with a living companion."

"He's not my slave. He's to become a Blood Drinker soon, only he's not yet been made," I improvised.

Ilio gazed up at me, his eyes wide, and I looked sharply back at him. *Hold your tongue, boy!* My glance said.

The old man said, "Ahh! Very interesting!" He turned to his entourage and informed them quickly of our exchange. The other elders, and even their guards, glanced meaningfully at one another.

I didn't like how this way going and was just about to seize Ilio and retreat when the old man bowed again and said, "But of course we have a dwelling where you may rest for the day. We are always honored to host the Potashu T'sukuru. Please follow us. We'll take you to a hut where you can recuperate from your journey."

For Ilio's sake, I followed the elder procession—though I was feeling less confident by the moment the boy might find a home here among the Ground Scratchers.

The people of the village stopped to stare as we passed, their eyes wide. It was obvious from the way they stared that I was not the first vampire they'd seen, but I could tell the sight was not a familiar one to them, or one that was particularly welcome. Although I could easily hear the words they whispered in a rush to one another, I could not yet decipher their language. I was starting to get a feel for the sentence structure and had picked up a couple basic nouns and verbs— the I's and You's and Is'es—but the rest was still gibberish to me.

As we walked, Chief Elder introduced his compatriots to us. "This is Hault, my Second-In-Command." Hault, a tall and regal man with a large hook nose, nodded to me gravely. "This is Y'vort, who is the eldest of us all. He is the One-Who-Speaks-With-Livia." Y'vort, a tiny and incredibly wrinkled creature, waved to me-- a frugal gesture, as if he was too old to waste much energy on petty social niceties. Y'vort had to be helped along by the third elder, who walked at his side, lightly gripping the older man's knobby elbow. "That is the elder Gant, who is Y'vort's son, and this is Ungst, the Chief-Master-of-the-Neirie." Ungst, the youngest of the elders, was a fat old boar with a thick mass of curly black hair and ornate scar patterns scrawled upon the entirety of his gross and hirsute body.

The toothless old chieftain named Bhulloch spoke to me in a brisk, glottal dialect, then switched back to Denghoi when he saw that I did not comprehend his speech. "You do not speak the tongue of the T'sukuru?" he asked sharply, his great bushy brows drawing together.

"I speak many languages, but they are mostly the languages of the northern climes. I do not come this far south very often, and I have difficulty with the tongue of the eastern T'sukuru tribes. I prefer speaking the tongue of the Denghoi."

The old man said, "Hmm..." My lies did not impress him.

Rod Redux

The dwelling they allotted us was large and finely appointed, with thick furs covering the ground and many hanging decorations. The lodging was suspiciously well-suited for a Blood Drinker's comfort: there was a circular interior chamber erected within the outer walls, with heavy draperies hanging in the doorway to block any light from falling through the entrance. It was dark as night inside, and there was no firepit or any type of opening in the roof to vent out smoke. Of course, a vampire would have no need for cooking fires. There was a single torch fluttering in the center of the room for light. I could literally feel my eyes twitch in relief, once the sun was no longer needling them mercilessly.

The Chief Elder bowed once more at the interior doorway and said, "Please consider yourselves our honored guests. You are welcome to stay as long as you require. Ungst will send food and drink for the boy. Have no worries, One-Called-Thest. You will be well guarded here in the village of the Oombai. You may continue your journey whenever you are rested, only come seek me before you leave. I humbly request an audience before you continue on your way... at your leisure, of course. The Oombai are ever content to serve the Potashu T'sukuru."

"You're most generous," I bowed.

The old man grinned, his eyes lingering on me a moment too long, then he let the door curtain drop into place.

"What does *Potashu T'sukuru* mean?" I asked Ilio, shouldering off my pack and dropping it against the wall.

The boy shrugged. "I'm not sure. *Susk* means feast in Dengoi."

I sighed and reclined on the ground. The furs were thick and soft. "Well, I hope you got an eyeful of their women, Ilio. I don't think we'll be staying here long. I don't like the cunning look in that old man's eyes. They want something from us... or from me. I'm sure of it. It was a mistake to come here."

I cast my eyes about the circular chamber, my nose crinkling. I smelled blood and death in here. Faint. Months old. And there was that unfamiliar odor again!

Ilio sat beside me. "The women here are very attractive. Are you sure we can't stay?"

I scowled at him. "I'd rather not."

"But you heard what they said about your people, Thest. The Oombai must trade with them regularly. Perhaps, we can meet them if we stay here. They might be able to help you find a way back to your wives and children."

I've been telling too many lies!

"Perhaps," I murmured, picking at a tuft of fur.

Before the boy could continue, three women pushed through the flap of the tent. The elder Ungst plodded in behind them, leering at us.

The women seemed hesitant to enter the chamber, their faces drawn with fear, their feet shuffling. The fat man prodded the women forward with a staff of polished wood, briefly annoyed.

"*Ne homh t'zwei Neirie,*" he said to us, his lascivious grin returning. "*Forst-ah t'shu?*"

When we gawped at him uncomprehendingly, he sighed and gestured with his hands. He made a circle with the thumb and first finger of his left hand, then sawed the forefinger of his right hand back and forth inside the circle. He laughed when he saw the understanding come into our eyes, then flapped his hand in our direction and departed.

Ilio's jaw had dropped to his chest when the servant women slipped quietly inside, their eyes averted. Even I, I must admit, was a little taken aback by their attractiveness.

They were naked save a scrap of leather about the waist. Their bodies were painted head to toe with a brilliant white cosmetic. There were patterns of concentric circles drawn around their breasts and navels, and glyphs and abstract markings on their faces, arms, and legs. Perhaps most strikingly, their hair was shorn near to the scalp, just a fuzz upon their heads, and heavy ornaments swung from their earlobes. They carried with them water gourds and broad shell bowls, all finely formed and decorated with crudely painted figures of animals and humans with exaggerated sexual organs.

We were clearly getting the five star treatment, if you'll pardon the anachronistic metaphor.

"We are your Neirie," the woman at the front said meekly. "We've been sent to attend to your comfort. You must forgive my sisters, most honored ones. I am the only one of us who speaks Denghoi."

Both of us sat up, Ilio at the sight of their nakedness, and I at the smell of their blood. I smiled as kindly as I could, motioning for them to attend to their duties. I made sure my fangs didn't show. I didn't want to frighten them any further than they were already scared, but my effort to look as non-threatening as possible made little impression on them. I could smell their anxiety. It oozed out of their pores in clouds.

The slave women moved demurely to serve us, pouring clear water in the polished shell bowls so they could bathe us. The eldest Neirie attended me, while her sisters looked after Ilio.

"Please, don't be afraid of me," I said to the woman as she kneeled and unlaced my leather shoes. "I won't harm you."

Her fingers slowed as she loosened the laces of my footwear, then she hurried back to her task. She kept her gaze averted as she relieved me of my clothing. She motioned for me to stand.

I accommodated her, ignoring the hunger burning in my belly, and stood naked as she washed me head to toe.

I heard the other women giggle and looked toward Ilio. He was standing naked as well, his pecker rigid as a cucumber.

One of the Neirie reached up with a wet cloth and washed it-- particularly well, I might add-- and his face turned red as an apple. Ilio's attendants peeked at one another evocatively, then let out another flourish of giggles.

I could tell by the tension in her shoulders that the woman attending to me was perturbed by her sisters' behavior. She shot them a scathing look, then moved around behind me and began to scrub my back.

"We are strangers to this region. Perhaps you can tell me why your people scratch at the ground as you do," I said as she washed my behind and the backs of my legs.

I didn't think she would respond to me at first, then she sighed and said, "They do it to turn the soil and make the vegetables grow. The old man says it pleases their Goddess."

"The One-Who-Speaks-With-Livia? The old one named Y'vort?"

"I do not believe in Livia. There is no goddess living in the soil. There is just dirt and worms and rocks."

I snorted. "My people share your skepticism. If there are gods, why do they never show themselves?"

"I thought the T'Sukuru claimed to be gods," the woman snapped, tossing her rag into the bowl. She rose and motioned for her sisters to follow her. "Do not think you will charm me with candor," she said, then she swept from the chamber with her sisters in tow.

5

Nonplussed, I moved to put my clothing back on. I dressed quickly and sat to slide my feet in my shoes, thinking all the while. Should we stay a little longer? Should we leave immediately? What secrets did the Elders possess, and what did they want from us?

I determined we should leave this place as soon as possible, but I was still mightily intrigued with the mystery of my vampire brethren. From what the slave girl said, they called themselves the T'sukuru, and portrayed themselves to be divine creatures. I wanted to know more. Perhaps she would return soon so I could question her further on the subject of those enigmatic blood drinkers. I did not trust to put many questions to the Elders. Their eyes were too greedy. I knew they sought advantage.

And what of Ilio?

I'd awakened to a strange and dangerous world. I had to educate myself if I were to secure my adopted son a prosperous new life. If this country was not suitable for the boy, then where should we settle?

Yes, I must know more.

The Neirie returned a short time later with food and drink for Ilio. At the sight of the women, the boy bolted upright. He was so anxious I feared my young companion would burst inside his breeches. The chamber already stank of his arousal. The boy's hormonal response to the women was stifling my ruminations, the scent overpowering all other smells in our lodging, but I knew there was little I could do to distract him. He was just of that age, the cusp of manhood. I shook my head, annoyed and amused.

This whole situation was exasperating.

What was I thinking, following the wishes of a horny young teenager? He knew nothing of the Oombai, only that his uncle had enthused about their women... and I, out of guilt, had capitulated to his wanderlust.

The Neirie plied the lad with food and drink. The smell of the liquid they served him was tart and somewhat rancid, like spoiled fruit. Face red, he gulped down the drink they poured for him, then with glistening chin, gestured greedily for more.

The eldest of the sisters returned to my side. She kneeled

quietly, awaiting my desires. She had a different air about her, as if she'd come to some new opinion of me, or decided on a different course of action. I smelled no fear coming from her now, though she was still tense.

"Tell me more about these other Blood Drinkers," I said to her.

She looked at me with a puzzled expression, meeting my eyes for the first time. "Do you know nothing of your own kind?" she asked.

I decided to be truthful. "I am from a faraway land and, in all honesty, I've never met another of my kind, aside from the one who made me what I am."

She searched my eyes before finally answering. "That is a dangerous ignorance, stranger, but what is there to tell?" She glanced toward her sisters, who were feeding Ilio by hand, laughing. "Their flesh is cold and hard as stone, just like yours. They come to the Oombai in the springtime, sometimes in the autumn, riding on the backs of great brutal animals. They come and they demand sacrifice, and the old fools give it to them. The Elders bow down and lick their feet, yet who can refuse them? The smallest of their number has the strength of ten men."

"How many are there, these Blood Drinkers, when they come?" I asked.

"Five, sometimes six. Their chieftain is a female with skin like volcanic glass. She's very beautiful, but cruel and full of spite. She calls herself Zenzele, and claims to be the goddess of death."

"And they take sacrifice?"

The woman nodded. "Sometimes three or four apiece before their wicked hunger is satisfied, then they move on to another village. The old men feed the Neirie to them. Never their own people."

"You were not born here?"

She scoffed. "You truly know nothing! No, I wasn't born here. Neirie is the Oombai word for 'taken'. I was stolen from my tribe when I was a young girl. My sisters and I were abducted as we played upon the shore of the lake our village sits beside. The Oombai send out parties each moon to steal the children of the other settlements, and no one is brave enough to oppose them because they are favored by the T'sukuru. If you declare war on the Oombai, you declare war on the Blood Drinkers they serve."

Across the room, Ilio was kissing the two serving girls passionately. Their ardor, I saw, was no less heated. He was uncharacteristically jolly. He was behaving, in fact, like someone drunk on *merje*, the psychotropic herb my people once used in fertility rituals and festivals.

"I think your... boy... has drank his fill," my Neirie companion said, a faint smile on her lips.

"I believe you're right," I nodded, laughing gently.

The Neirie turned to me then, a strange look in her eyes.

"I know you take refreshment of another sort, T'sukuru," she murmured. I met her gaze—she was a frail beauty, with large blue eyes—and I felt a sudden stirring for her, a powerful desire, not for her blood, but for her body... the desire a living man might feel. I was suddenly very confused, anxious even, as if I were feeling these stirrings for the first time. Well, it had been seven thousand years since I'd been intimate with a woman. You have to cut me a little slack here!

"My name is Aioa. You may sup of my blood, if it pleases you." As she spoke, she held out her delicate wrist.

"My name is Thest," I replied, and I even swallowed in nervousness, again as a living man might do.

She nodded, moving closer to me. "Have you made love to a woman since becoming T'sukuru?" she asked.

I shook my head no.

Her wrist, I saw, was heavily scarred. The scars

crisscrossed her flesh, extending halfway up her arm to her elbow. Was she accustomed to feeding her blood to others of my kind? Her wounds would seem to confirm that, but the idea offended me. I'm a predator, not some filthy leech!

The smell of her body confused me. She was frightened, yes, but also aroused. I could smell the moisture between her thighs. Her nipples were erect. Yet her heart was racing in her breast, and not from lust. She knew what she offered me was dangerous for her, so why then did she do it? Did she seek to make an alliance with me? Did she think I could be swayed?

She peeked at me beneath her eyebrows and murmured, "Please, be gentle with me, Thest."

"Do you want me to drink your blood, or do you want to mate with me?" I asked. I was horrified by the former... but mightily tempted to try the latter. Far too tempted for this woman's safety.

"Aren't you thirsty?" she inquired.

I pushed her arm down. "I'm sorry, little one. I have no control of my predatory instincts. I fear I would do more than sip."

I saw her eyes flash, alarmed by my words, then she gathered her courage and said, "I don't believe you will hurt me. You are not like the other ones."

I peeked at her proffered wrist again. All those scars.

"You... you have offered yourself to others of my kind? Allowed them to drink from your veins?"

"A couple times, when the Elders demanded it of me."

"And have the Elders demanded it of you this day?"

She smiled. "No. They don't know yet what to make of you."

I glanced toward Ilio, who was guzzling down more of the rancid fruit juice as the Nierie women stroked his chest and tugged the shoes off his feet. He was certainly offering them no resistance!

My resolve weakened and I took her wrist and brought it to my lips. I bared my fangs so that she could see them, gave her a moment to withdraw, but instead of changing her mind, her eyes narrowed, and the muscles in her face grew tense, as if with lust. I could smell the chemicals of her sexual arousal, a musky mélange, and the last of my restraint dissolved. She yelped as I bit into her flesh and then her blood was on my lips, spurting across my tongue. Pleasure shot through me in hot, pulsing bolts. Aioa gasped and shivered as I swallowed, then I drew another mouthful from her wrist.

"Oh! Not so hard!" she pleaded.

No creature in this world, neither man nor beast, had ever offered me their willing blood ... or took such pleasure in my feeding from them, but this Neirie, this fragile beauty named Aioa, twisted her body and gasped in pleasure as I drank from her.

Her hot, salty blood throbbed in my mouth. The smell and taste of it struck every nerve in my maw like a bolt of lightning, her heart a drum beat in my ears, the smell of her in my nostrils, the finest fragrance in the world right then. It seemed the flickering torchlight in the hut turned red and began to throb as I sucked her lifeblood inside me.

Ilio moaned in pleasure and I turned my eyes, my lips still latched to Aioa's wrist, to see him mating with the other two Neirie. At last, my son becomes a man! I would have laughed were my mouth not full of blood.

"My blood gives rise to your manhood," Aioa murmured, eyeing the bulge in the front of my trousers. "Would you let me please you in both matters at once?"

Grinning, I loosened the laces of my breeches and wriggled half out of them.

Aioa threw her thighs across mine and settled onto my manhood. I felt my cock pierce her, slide moistly in her heat. Her mouth gaped as I penetrated her. I opened my legs and she wriggled me deeper inside. Her blood overspilled my mouth and ran, hot and wet, down my neck and chest.

She pulled her wrist away to press her breasts together in pleasure, smearing blood all over them. She yelped as I stabbed my organ up in her, as I pulled her to me and licked the blood from her swollen nipples.

Some vampires will claim that sex pales in comparison to the pleasure of drinking blood, but I have a sneaking suspicion that the ones who do so have never had intercourse after their transformation. Though I've not often enjoyed the act of lovemaking throughout the millennia—it is so very, very dangerous for the human partner-- I have always considered both acts equally fine. Yet, I've encountered no other earthly pleasure the equal of the thing I've come to call the Blood Orgasm. That day, in the village of the Oombai, I experienced my first Blood Orgasm, and so it stands out in my memories, singular in its power to move me to lust.

Aioa put the tender flesh of her wrist back to my lips and I sucked, thrusting hard into the damp cleft between her thighs. I sucked her blood and thrust into her, over and over, until the pleasure of tongue and cock reached its inevitable climax. I howled as my manhood pumped vampiric cum inside her cunt, as her blood spurted in my mouth. Her pussy clenched down as tight as a fist and then it began to quiver around me, her bloody tits pressed to my cheeks, her fingers in my hair, pulling hard. I don't know how she survived, how I managed not to kill her, only that pleasure must have tempered my savagery, that I was too enraptured in the ecstasy pulsing through my body to incline from lust to violence. Perhaps her frailty spoke to the gentler man inside me, the one who always fights against the hunger.

"Whahudd!" Aioa cried, and she pushed herself away from me, out of my lap and off my manhood. She fell on her back weakly, sprawling between my open thighs, her head lolling, her breasts heaving. Blood pattered on the furs beneath her, still gouting from her wounded wrist, but weaker now— I'd drained so much of it.

Her Neirie sisters moved to attend her (Ilio having spent himself quickly with them) and they dipped their fingers into her sex, taking my black, sterile seed and dabbing it onto the gashes in her wrist.

I watched in mute amazement as my undead ejaculate sealed the wound in her wrist, stitching it closed almost instantly. The flesh around the injury swelled—appearing for an instant as if it were a badly infected injury-- and then rapidly the swelling subsided and the edges of the bites melted together until the wound my teeth had sliced into her flesh was just another winding scar.

I looked to Ilio, and he returned my dumbfounded gaze.

Panting, Aioa sat up. She brushed aside her sisters and smiled at me. "Never have I felt such pleasure," she declared breathlessly, shaking her head to clear it. She cut her eyes toward the doorway then, and leaned forward to confide, "I would be killed for telling you this, T'sukuru. Be mindful of the life I entrust in your care. The chieftain Bhulloch sent me to you as an enticement. It has been too long since your brethren have visited the Oombai. The Elders need the *ebu potashu* or the years they have cheated will catch up with them. If you do not give it to them, they will try to take it by force. I overheard the Chief Elder commanding his warriors. He told them you and your boy are not to leave the village." She grinned wickedly and finished her betrayal in a whisper, speaking fast lest she be overheard. "They're cruel masters, T'sukuru. I say let them die. Let them die and rot in *Hal'eh'far*!"

I shook my head. I was having trouble following her. Too many of her words were foreign to me. "What is this 'ebu potashu'?"

"The blood!" Aioa hissed. "The black blood! I've seen your

kind spit it up for the Elders. The old pigs lick it up like dogs who eat their own vomit. It makes them live when they should be food for worms! You truly are an outcast, aren't you?"

I found myself hypnotized by this woman, so beautiful and fragile, yet so secretly full of passion. Her fury reminded of my second wife Nyala. My head swam with the old memories, and the afterglow of our heated lovemaking. I felt swayed by her allure, my black heart tugged by the female staring fiercely into my eyes, tugged as the moon tugs the seas, the invisible but powerful tides of attraction.

I did not fear the old man Bhulloch. I could slaughter the whole village on a whim. My only real vulnerability was Ilio.

"I will leave then," I said, pulling up my pants and tucking my flaccid cock away. "I will leave them to their natural dissolution, and come back with the night to take you with me, if that is something that you wish."

"Not now!" she hissed. "There are too many guards. They surround this lodge at his commands, and are spread throughout the village, too. Bhulloch has instructed them to kill you if you try to escape, or kill the boy in failing that. Wait until it is night and their warriors are blinded by the dark."

She did not know my strength, obviously. I had survived the maw of a glacier, a mountain of grinding ice. Yet, I worried for Ilio, who was mortal. I could not move at full speed with him in my arms. The force would kill him, and all it would take was one lucky spear or arrow to end his life.

Perhaps... perhaps a trade. The three Neirie women and a peaceful departure in exchange for a bit of my immortal spittle.

It seemed like a fair bargain, one the Elders would leap at.

"Why do you tell me these things?" I asked. It was my final suspicion. "You risk your life for us, yet we are strangers to you."

The woman named Aioa drew herself up. "I was not born

a slave, Blood Drinker," she said haughtily. "If I had the strength of your kind, I would kill those old men and end the rule of the wicked Oombai, once and for all."

Then she seemed to fear she'd said too much. She motioned curtly to her sisters and they rose. Heads down, the three of them departed.

6

After they left, Ilio dozed, drunk on the rancid fruit drink the Neirie had plied him with. He snored naked on his back, a satisfied smile upon his lips. I remained wary, my mind restless with anxiety. I was a stranger in a strange land. The customs of these Ground Scratchers, these people called the Oombai, were outrageous to my sensibilities. Had the entire world advanced in such a manner during my long sleep in the ice? This culture seemed little better than the Foul Ones who had bedeviled my race so long ago. I longed for the simplicity of my mountain cave, and the tranquility of my long solitude there, overlooking the valley of my human life, with only the wind and the bones of my loved ones, long buried, to keep me company.

What should I do with Ilio? My adopted child was a vulnerability. My vampire flesh might be nigh impregnable, but my heart was not so unassailable. Ilio, as much as I loved him, was a chink in my natural defenses, a weakness I had not accounted for.

Perhaps I should transform him into an immortal. I thought I knew the trick of it. It had been performed on me, after all. It seemed simple enough-- the transfer of the Living Blood. An instant of writhing agony, and then...

But I loved the boy. I loved his humanity. His innocence. My offenses against him were numerous enough. Did I dare make them insurmountable?

The Oldest Living Vampire on the Prowl

As I mulled these thoughts in my mind, afternoon melted into evening. Ilio rose from his nap and wanted to venture outside. He was eager to explore the village of the Oombai. He'd glimpsed innumerable curiosities when we passed through the avenues of the settlement earlier, and with the recklessness of naiveté, he wanted to investigate each of them further. He'd paid little attention to my conversation with Aioa. In his youth, and in his assurance of my strength, he thought us invulnerable, the menace of the Elders' schemes a petty concern. Before I could counsel him otherwise, impress on him the gravity of our situation, the curtain of the hut was swept aside and Elder Bhulloch ducked inside.

"I trust you've rested well, Thest. Evening has come, which I know is more to the liking of your people. Come. Accompany me to the plaza. We've prepared a feast in your honor. I think you'll find it entertaining."

He rubbed his hands together as we rose.

"Come! Come!" Bhulloch pressed us. "The weather is pleasant. Let us enjoy ourselves tonight."

His guards fell into step behind us as we accompanied the bent old man to the sprawling community's central court.

"This way. This way," the old man said.

I assessed the warriors as we walked. They were armed with spears and knives and were heavily muscled, their faces grim. It was obvious Bhulloch's escort was a pair of veteran warriors. Their bodies were darkened by the elements and crisscrossed with a multitude of scars. They had seen battle. They would kill without hesitation. No danger to me, of course. I was ready to pounce at the slightest provocation. But I worried for Ilio, who trotted along at my side without a care, enthusiastic, commenting loudly at all the wonders he beheld.

"Look at the torches!" he gasped. "I've never seen so many torches, Thest! It is night, yet the village is bright as day!"

The central plaza was an arrangement of low curved walls.

Rod Redux

The walls were constructed of stone, their size and shape carefully selected so that the structure was uniform and aesthetically pleasing. The ramparts were organized in several concentric circles, within which the elite of Oombai society had gathered, sitting upon low benches made of flat river rocks, their bottoms cushioned with woven mats or furs. The Neirie tended dutifully to their masters, cooling them with ornate feather fans or fetching food and drink for them. It seemed to me the further we traveled within the crude amphitheater, the richer and older the Oombai grew as we passed.

The buzz of their conversations made my ears throb. The smell of their bodies was overwhelming. I felt my mouth water as the blood hunger stirred inside me, but I wrestled it down. It would be Ilio's death if I lost control.

I cast out with my senses for the Neirie named Aioa. She was near. I could smell her... There! I spied her attending one of the elders in the central circle, the fat one named Ungst, the slave master. She was pouring wine for him while he squeezed her ass, ignoring the crude laughter he shared with his companions.

Ilio gasped. "Thest! Look!"

I turned my eyes and beheld a curious sight. Standing upon the central dais was a nude male with skin so dark it was almost black. The man was moving his hands rhythmically, catching and throwing several sizzling torches in the air. Always there was one flaming torch twirling in the air above his head, and he continued this act without dropping any of them as Bhulloch showed us to our seats.

"Please, sit at my right, Thest. It is the seat of honor," he said.

This was a great festival, greater than any I had ever enjoyed. As Neirie summoned steaming platters of food for Ilio and my hosts to gorge themselves on, I found a gourd of blood pressed into my hands. I sniffed the contents of the cup.

It was fresh human blood. But who did this blood belong to? I brought it to my lips. Still warm...!

"Drink! Drink!" Bhulloch cried.

As the feast progressed, the entertainment waxed even more outlandish. After the juggler, a group of nude performers entertained the crowds by walking on their hands or contorting their bodies into boneless-looking shapes. Tumblers took great leaps—great by human standards, anyway—spinning their bodies in the air before rolling back to their feet to do it again. We were entertained by limber female dancers, whose bellies undulated sinuously, writhing rapidly in and out. They alternately concealed and exposed their nakedness behind great fans of fluttering feathers as they made their way around the central circle, grinding their genitals, which were spread open by piercings, in the faces of the elite. As the Oombai select grew increasingly drunk, they cried out for sexual performances, something or someone they called Halforeh Tapas. I watched as a massively endowed male was hauled onto the stage, a sturdy leash knotted round his neck. He was a giant, nearly seven foot tall, with a wild red mane and a body covered in a wiry, animalistic pelt of curly hair. His attendants threatened him with clubs, pointing him toward a waiting female. To the crowd's screams of approval, he mated with the pale and buxom woman, one of the feather dancers. The big man's cock seemed almost too massive to fit inside the woman's body. I could see the female straining to accommodate him. After he spilled his seed inside her, animals were led onto the dais then and the couplings on display became even more debased, for the beasts did not mate with other animals, but bleated and squalled as they were sullied by Neirie males. Though the cheering and laughter grew even louder, I found the sight repulsive.

I sought to engage the chieftain Bhulloch in conversation, but he was distracted by the copulations on the dais. He eyed the vulgar displays with an expression of voracious jealousy. I wanted to know more about the vampires who traded with his people, but he did not heed my subtle hints, and then I was distracted myself as Ilio—too full on drink and the rich, greasy food he'd stuffed himself on—doubled over and began to vomit on the ground between his feet.

Bhulloch noticed the boy puking and laughed merrily. "Your slave runneth over!" he wheezed.

"You've had enough," I said sternly to the boy when his convulsions had passed. I snatched the fruit out of his hands and threw it aside.

Ilio wiped his lips and nodded. His face was red and snot was hanging from his nostrils. "I'm sorry, Thest."

When the final goat had been defamed and the plundered beasts were led back to their pens, Bhulloch sought to engage me in conversation.

It had grown late and many of the festival-goers were stumbling drunkenly to their homes. The torches were burning low. The plaza was emptying. I was relieved the time for bargaining had come. My patience was long past frayed.

The old man, his eyes rimmed red by the rancid fruit drink he'd gulped all night, came to the point nearly without preamble, emboldened by his drunkenness. His health was waning, he told me. He woke in the morning coughing blood, and had begun to pass blood in his shit as well. The Oombai knew my peoples' blood had healing properties. They called the magic blood *ebu potashu*, and paid a handsome price for it when the T'sukuru came to trade. What prize, he asked, could he offer to entice me to impart some of my curative *potash*?

Of course, I was ready for the old beggar. "I will give you what you seek, Old One. I ask only one favor in return."

"What is that?" the old man inquired eagerly. He clasped his hands together, as if to restrain himself from embracing me.

"The Neirie who attended us today in our hut…"

"Yes?"

"I desire the one called Aioa."

The old man grinned, exposing his two rotten teeth. "Ahh! Yes! Yes! The fiery one has sparked your desire, has she? I'm happy to be rid of her, to be truthful. And such a small favor to ask! You are far more reasonable than your brethren from the East. They demand too much, and offer so little in return."

He gestured with a finger, commanding his attendants in the Oombai's gibberish tongue. His Neirie nodded and hurried through the thinning crowd to fetch the fiery-tempered slave girl.

The other elders had gathered round, their eyes gleaming hungrily. A large shell bowl was placed on the ground at my feet. A receptacle for my *potashu*... or so I believed.

There is no such thing as a small favor, I thought to myself. I will give them just a little, and use their desire for more to bargain for Aioa's sisters as well.

The Elders' greedy eyes made me uncomfortable. I cast my thoughts inwards, to the cold black thing that resided within me. I remembered how my maker had transformed me. How he opened his fanged jaws and caused the black blood inside him to pour into my mouth. I had vomited many times in my life, when I was still human and vulnerable to illness. Surely it was not much different.

As I contemplated the act, I saw that Aioa was being led by Bhulloch's attendants toward our group. Why was she balking? Surely she wanted to be free!

"Bring that obstinate creature over here!" Bhulloch commanded. He spoke some more in Oombai, waving with a curled finger. Aioa was pressed to her knees in front of me. I tried to catch her eye, to smile at her, thinking she would be pleased that I had won her freedom, but when I did, I saw that her eyes were round with horror. I realized too late the old man had misunderstood me.

Before I could protest, the attendant behind her pulled her chin up by the bristles of her head and sliced her throat open with a blade.

"No!" I cried.

Aioa twitched and made choking sounds as the attendant drained her blood into the bowl, holding her head in his hands. She batted the air. Struck the edge of the bowl. Almost overturned it.

"No-no-no!" I roared, leaping to my feet. I shoved the attendant who'd butchered her away from the dying woman. In my horror, I used my full strength, and the man went flying across the amphitheater. He sailed clear over the central dais and collided with the stone wall on the other side with enough force to topple a section of it. He slumped to the ground, blood drooling from his mouth, the bones in his back and pelvis shattered.

I thought to use my vampire blood to save the woman, but before I could move to do so, the elders fell away in fear and their guards swarmed forward to attack me.

I snarled and fell to one knee as a quiver of arrows plunged into my shoulder and ribs, converging on me from several directions at once.

Bhulloch tried to scramble away, his mouth agape, his eyes bulging, but Gant and his ancient sire stood in his path.

In fury and pain, I lashed out at the Chief Elder. The top of his head exploded amidst the pale blurred sweep of my arm. Brains and blood and chunks of flesh peppered the mass of panicked humans surrounding us. The old man's body slid down, the top half of it missing. All that remained of his face was a jaw, hanging askew, and the wet pink worm of his tongue.

Ilio cried out then, and I turned to see him falling onto his hip, the shaft of an arrow protruding from his breast. A second arrow whistled toward him, but I managed to snatch it from the air before it found his throat.

I roared as my maker had roared that day on the mountain, when we went to confront the monster plaguing the Neanderthals. An expanding ring of dust swirled from the ground around me. Many of the encircling torches guttered out. To my left, the surviving elders clutched their heads, the tall one Hault stumbling to his knees. To my right, blood burst from Ilio's nose and ears. My howl had ruptured his eardrums.

Ilio! His safety was my only thought then. My adopted son had been wounded!

I scooped him into my arms. Several Oombai warriors were sprinting toward us, brandishing spears and knives. Holding the boy tight to my body, I fled as fast as I dared to move. I leapt to the raised dais in the center of the piazza, and bound from there up and over the heads of the fleeing humans. Several more arrows hissed through the air as I accelerated, but I leapt clear of them. They all passed harmlessly beneath me... all save one, which flew at me from the rear, where I could not see it. This bolt, a sling-thrown javelin, pierced the meaty part of my upper hip. It struck with enough force to turn me in the air, but I did not lose hold of the boy, and clutching Ilio tight to me, I leapt clear of the plaza and crossed the village of the Ground Scratchers in moments, the little thatch huts blurring past.

Ilio moaned into the cold skin of my neck as I flew through the air with him. The wind flattened his hair to his brow. He coughed blood against my shoulder. He tried to speak but the roar of the wind snatched his words from his lips.

Stars and moon overhead. The village behind us. The great plains stretching out ahead.

Let me find a copse of wood where I could tend to his wounds...!
"Don't die, boy!" I commanded.

My feet touched earth and I leapt again into the whistling air.

Interval

Liege. December 24, 2010. 3:32 am.

For a moment, I sat on the edge of the bed, my eyes distant. I was still far away in my thoughts, far from my finely appointed apartment with all its modern amenities: its televisions and laptop computer, its telephone and security system, electric refrigeration unit and cooktop range (these very rarely used). The wail of a police siren drifted very faintly into the room from the street below, but I did not hear it. For a moment I was still flying across that Austrian plain, my dying child in my arms, an arrow piercing him between the ribs. I was still fleeing through the night, looking for a safe wooded place where we could hide from the Oombai long enough for me to tend to the boy's injuries.

Then the man taped to the chair across the room from me shifted in his bindings and cleared his throat, and I blinked, my mind returning to the present. My gleaming eyes tilted his direction, and I smiled.

"Do you have children, Mister…? Ah! I just realized I do not know your surname. What is your family name, Lukas?"

My handsome captive answered my smile with a sullen grimace. "Jaeger," he finally replied.

"Jaeger," I repeated, a look of amusement crossing my stony features. "Do you know the origin of your surname, Mr. Jaeger?" I asked.

Rod Redux

"No."

"Jaeger means 'huntsman'."

He just stared at me.

"I thought you would be amused by the coincidence," I said, but he appeared unmoved. "Ah well. You modern folk have little respect for such things. Too much TV. All the noise and flashing images atrophy your sense of wonder."

I have little patience for television. With my enhanced senses, I can see the images as they are inscribed on the surface of the display, one by one, like cartoon pictures in a child's animated flipbook. It gives me a headache.

I do, however, enjoy music. I have fine collections of vinyl recordings in all my far flung homes. The collection I have in my American home is quite self-indulgent, I must confess. I have a lot of time to pursue my hobbies.

I thought of my rambling estate in the Appalachian Mountains, near the Cherokee National Forest in Northeastern Tennessee. The mountains there are so beautiful in the summer. It is tranquil and remote. I should return there soon. It's been a long time.

Excuse me. I'm so easily distracted...!

"As I was saying..." I continued. "Tell me, Mr. Jaeger, do you have children?"

My captive—my beautiful killer, my plunderer, my rapist—did not respond to my question at first. I could see the thoughts running through his mind. How should he reply? With the truth? With a lie? What would benefit him the most? And why was I asking him this? Was I probing for weakness, something I could threaten him with?

Finally, reluctantly, he nodded.

I sighed. "A boy," I said. I could see it in the way his eyes and mouth moved.

He shot me a startled glance. "Yes," he said.

"What is his name?"

"I'm not telling you that!"

I spread my hands. It didn't matter. "I have no desire to harm your child. I was merely curious," I said.

Rising from my seat, I drifted toward the balcony doors. I pushed aside the heavy drapes and looked out at the city. The glass was frosted, the skyline blurred by the intricate crystal patterns. "I only wondered if you would understand what I did next. If you could fathom the horror I felt as my adopted son lay dying in my arms. I loved him, though he was no child of my flesh. The thought of losing him was too much for me to bear. And so, once again, I found myself heaping another great wickedness onto the pile of offenses I had already committed against the boy. All of them sins of my own immeasurable egotism. He was ever, and always remained, an innocent, unsullied by my depravities. Even when he rose up against me, his vengeance was pure."

I felt tears come to my eyes. I stood with my back to my captive, my vision blurring for a moment. Not human tears. Of course not. These were the cold, infectious black tears of a monster. Ebu potashu, in the language of the Oombai. The Black Blood. My vampire lover Zenzele called it the Venom.

I did not wish the brute to see my pain. I wiped the tears away quickly.

"So you turned him into a vampire," Lukas said.

"Yes, of course, I did," I murmured.

The man shifted in his seat again. I knew he was dreadfully uncomfortable, but I wasn't about to release him. He was, after all, my captive audience. Call it "dinner theatre".

All joking aside, I was still in the mood to reminisce.

"Listen, Varney," the German said. "I want to hear the rest of your story. I really do, but right now I need to piss like a racehorse. I'm about to bust."

I couldn't help myself. I burst out laughing.

I was tempted to let him soil himself, but then, angry and

humiliated, what kind of audience would he be? And I wanted him to hear my tale of woe.

What is a story without a listener?

Answer: The masturbation of the literate.

Without replying, other than my surprised laugh, I turned and left the room. In my kitchenette, I flipped through the cabinets. There were few dishes, little in the way of food-- only enough to maintain the appearance of normality, if, by some chance, I might have guests who would look through my cupboards.

"What are you doing?" my captive asked when I returned to my bed chamber.

He protested as I kneeled down before him and tugged at the zipper of his fine designer pants.

"Hey! Stop that! Don't!" he objected, his face blazing red. He kicked and jerked in his chair, trying to squirm away from me.

"Calm yourself," I scolded him. "You said you needed to urinate."

"Yes, but--!"

"But what?" I asked mildly. "Did you expect me to release you from your bonds? Allow you to roam free in my home? On your honor? A child murderer?" I chuckled. "You would lunge for the nearest sharp object, I'm certain. Not that it would do you any good."

Flushed and sweating, he set his features in an expression of resigned indignation, turned his face aside. At his acquiescence, I wriggled his fly the rest of the way down and slid my fingers inside the gap. He jerked a little at my icy touch. His organ grew slightly tumescent as I handled it, but I pretended I didn't notice. He had a rather large penis. I could smell the little girl still on it, the child he had murdered after raping tonight. Placing his uncircumcised cock inside the rim of a large drinking glass, I waited for him to void his bladder.

I watched as his face turned ever ruddier. Finally, he said in a strangled voice: "I can't."

"Shall I avert my gaze?" I mocked him.

He glared at me, suddenly enraged. I watched the veins in his neck and temples stand out, and then a great gush of urine sprayed from his cock.

"There we go," I chortled. "You really had to go. You've almost filled it up."

I left the room when he was finished and poured his vile-smelling urine into the commode. I flushed. Glanced at the soiled tumbler and dropped it into the garbage can.

He glared at me with pure hatred when I returned, sitting with his knees splayed and his cock dangling out his fly. "What if I have to do number two?" he asked.

I arched an eyebrow. "I trust you'll not press your luck so soon."

He grinned wickedly.

"My hunger for your blood is very finely balanced against my desire to converse tonight," I warned him.

I walked to him, helped him regain his dignity, then left one more time to wash my hands. I did not want his rapist's stench on my flesh.

When I had taken my seat on the edge of the bed across from him, he prompted me: "So… you turned the kid into a vampire."

I smiled sadly, my eyes waxing distant. "Yes. Ilio was my first Blood Child." I looked down at my hands, clasped once more between my knees. "In all the millennia I'd lived as a vampire, I never thought to make another like me. The idea, in truth, never even crossed my mind. That was how much I hated the monster I'd become. But he was dying, my young Ilio, my innocent little boy, and I was weak. I could not bear to let him go."

The Raising of a Dead Child

1

I could smell the blood pouring out of him, but worse than that, I could smell the life pouring out of him. Every moment I delayed, my adopted child emptied of blood... and filled up with death. I was out of my mind with despair and anger. He had so little time left--!

Love was probably the only thing which kept me from succumbing to my appetite. I felt no temptation to drink the boy's blood as I fled across the plains, despite the fact that I was covered in the oozing, hot fluid. My clothes were soaked with it. It blew off my body in whirling droplets, falling to the grass below in a scant and horrid rain. But in my love for the boy, I had no desire to drink it. I did not even think of such a thing.

I thought only of my love for the boy as I shot through the moonlit heavens. I thought only of saving him.

As I angled toward the haven of a darkened copse of pine, well away from the menace of the Oombai, I promised myself vengeance on those greedy, wicked elders. If my young charge passed into the afterlife, they would join him shortly.

Yes! I swore to myself. If Ilio died, I would return and slaughter them all!

I would extinguish their race like a mad white god.

I would bathe in a river of corpses!

I arced through the night with the boy in my arms. The plains rushed up to me. My feet touched the earth and I slowed the speed of my movement as gently as I could. The moon flickered behind a lattice of tree branches and foliage. I glided within the shadows of the copse and laid Ilio on a soft hump of grass and fallen pine needles.

Ilio's eyes rolled toward me. He was pale, shivering.

The crickets, which had fallen silent at our arrival, resumed their nightly choir. I made quick work of my injuries. Gritting my teeth, I yanked the arrows from my flesh, giving no thought to the pain or the black blood rising within the wounds to erase them from existence. With a snarl, I wrenched the javelin from my rump and tossed it in the underbrush.

"Thest," my adopted son murmured, "It hurts."

He coughed and blood seeped from the corner of his lips.

"Hush, now, boy," I said sternly. "Let me tend to your wounds."

I sat back on my knees and examined the arrow protruding from his ribs. It was so deep! Did I dare pull it out?

Of course, I knew what I had to do. I could smell death on his tremulous exhalations. I had but a moment. Make him immortal... or allow him to die.

My motives required no deeper examination. I was weak. I could not lose him as I'd lost my human family, so many ages ago.

"I think I'm dying," Ilio sputtered. "Stay with me til it's over, Thest. It's dark here. I'm... scared."

"You don't have to die, boy. I can heal you. I can make you like me." I spoke quickly, brushing his bangs back from his brow. "It will hurt, but you will rise from this place an immortal being."

Did he nod, or was it only my imagination? Foolish monster--! Foolish, careless monster--!

His eyelids fluttered. The boy's eyes rolled up white. Panicked, I opened his jaws with my fingers and leaned over his face, moving my mouth over his, our lips just a centimeter apart. I did then by instinct the thing that my maker had done to me, so many eons ago. I summoned the black blood from inside me—the Venom, the Demon, the Strix—and I poured it into his mouth.

It rose from within like an angry living thing, clawing its way out of the altered cells of my tissue, uncoiling itself from my internal organs. The pain was stark and tearing. It felt like I was being ripped inside out.

With a convulsive croak, the *ebu potashu* poured from my lips, an ebon gout of fibrous tissue and fluid, thick and syrupy and stinking. Ilio's lips and cheeks were painted black. His mouth filled up with it. Then, as if by some trick of light, it seemed to rear up in his maw and plunge straight down his gullet.

He shot upright, clawing at his throat.

His eyes locked to mine, bulging with terror and pain.

"It will last only a moment," I promised, falling back from him weakly. I scooted a couple feet away, clutching my stomach. "Be brave!"

I watched, helpless, as the boy jerked back, then began to writhe and twist on the ground, sobbing and crying out as the living hunger worked its way through his veins. I relived my own transformation as I watched him shudder and claw in agony at the ground beneath him. Sympathetic pain worked its way through my limbs as he contorted.

I remembered the charnel pit where my vampire father imprisoned me, the ground piled with his stiff, frozen victims. I remembered the way the monster had come to steal my humanity, dropping down through the entrance of the pit like a great bird of prey, his fur cloak spread out around him. He took me by force, the wicked creature, prized my lips open and vomited the foul black blood into my mouth. And the pain. I remembered the horrible, engulfing pain... how it spread through my veins in burning cold threads, devouring all that was human in me, turning me into a thing of ice and hunger.

"Ilio... Ilio, I'm sorry," I gasped.

His body went taut, his back arching up. His spine bent so far I feared it would snap. The shaft in his ribs quivered, then he collapsed. His head lolled on his neck like a flower with a broken stem.

He stopped breathing. His eyes went blank, staring into the black forest, staring into the blackness of death.

The spark of life had left him.

"Ilio...?"

I choked back a sob, scrubbing my eyes. *Too late--!*

Then I saw his flesh begin to whiten. I dared to hope.

The transformation spread slowly from the center of his body, working down his arms, his hands, down to the very tips of his fingers. His nails turned to glass. His bronze skin faded to the color of bone. His face became a sculpture of gleaming marble. His glazed eyes glimmered, then blinked, then rolled toward me. For a moment, they caught the moonlight, and his pupils filled with gibbous light. It was beautiful and horrible all at the same time.

"I live," he murmured, his voice full of disbelief. Then he smiled and I saw his eyeteeth elongating.

2

The shaft was still sticking out of him. I shifted toward him as he sat up. "Let me get that arrow out of you," I said. He nodded, and I put my hand on his chest and yanked the bolt out. He winced but did not cry out. Pulling his shirt open, he examined his torso. Though he was covered in tacky blood, the wound had begun to vanish. He looked at me with wonder.

"Yes," I said with a chuckle. "Your injuries will heal quickly now."

He touched the place where the arrow had wounded him, sketching his fingers over his ribs, but of his mortal injury, there was no trace. Not even a scar.

"Come," I said. "Let us rise. We must find a place to hide before daylight comes. I fear the Oombai will send their warriors after us."

I put my hand on the boy's elbow and helped him to his feet. As he rose, he bent forward with a gasp, clutching his guts. "Oh! My stomach! It hurts!"

"I know. I've afflicted you with my hunger for blood. I'm sorry."

He blinked at me, confused and in pain.

"Come," I said. "We need to move quickly. I will help you feed and then we must find shelter."

We walked quickly from the dark of the wood, out into the moonlit plains. The grass hissed as the wind tilted earthward and blew across the low hills. As we travelled side by side, I educated him. "You're a Blood Drinker, now," I said. "There is a demon inside you that ravens for the life fluid of the living, but it grants you strength in return. Strength and speed and the ability to heal rapidly. All this, so you may hunt your prey more easily. Your senses have been sharpened, your thoughts and reflexes quickened. I've made you a god, but I've also cursed you."

"For love," he said, and I nodded.

"I could not bear to let you die."

He nodded, looking at me with awe... with awe and abject adulation. His flesh seemed to glow in the moonlight, as if there was a nimbus of light surrounding him.

"I can see every lash in your eyelids," he said then. He squinted. "Every wrinkle in your lips. Every—"

I put my hand up with a chuckle. "One of the first things

you must learn to do, boy, is try and block all that out. It serves only to distract. Your senses will overwhelm you if you allow them to. You must be the master of them, and not let them rule you."

Ilio glanced away, frowning in concentration. "Yes. Yes, I will try."

I turned my face south, toward the country of the Ground Scratchers. We'd traveled a couple kilometers in my brief, mad flight. I stretched out with my senses then, searching for pursuers. Yes, the hunters were coming! A large group of them. I could hear the distant babble of their voices, angry and vengeful.

Foolish men, I thought. I recalled the face of the slave woman Aioa. I would teach them about vengeance!

If I'd already tested the strength of my vampire child, I would have set us against our pursuers, but I did not know yet how powerful Ilio had become. I had not trained him in the use of his new skills. I could not risk a confrontation… not yet.

Turning away, I said, "Let us see how powerful and swift you have become. Follow me."

With that, I flung myself into the wind.

I flew at about half the speed I could actually summon. As if launched from a catapult, my body rose silently into the sky in a smooth, controlled arc. I landed near an alder one hundred meters to the north and turned around to watch the boy.

I could see Ilio, small now with distance. I watched him crouch down and throw himself into the sky.

He landed well short of me. Tripped. Rolled across the grass. He rose and leapt again. This time, he travelled much further, the arc of his leap higher than his first attempt. I watched him descend from the sky toward me, flapping his arms and legs, his eyes wide and frightened.

I moved out of the way. He crashed into the foliage of the

alder, vanishing from sight with a swish and the crunch of breaking branches. An instant later, he dropped from the boughs with a thump.

I rushed to his side, trying to restrain my mirth. "Are you hurt?" I asked.

My careless new vampire child sat up with a strangled cry. A splintered tree branch was sticking out of his belly.

I kneeled down beside him and pulled the broken limb from his abdomen. He healed, but his healing was nowhere near the speed at which my injuries vanished. "Before you leap, you should take heed of where you're going to land," I scolded him gently.

Ilio nodded. "Yes, Thest."

He looked embarrassed. I ruffled his hair.

"Have no shame. You'll catch the trick of it," I said. "I flailed about like a buffoon the first night I was a Blood Drinker. Your body has been transformed, but your mind is still a human mind. You will discover your strength and a wealth of new talents, but it will take time for your human mind to take ownership of them. You're like a child who must learn to walk again. You will fall many times before you can run."

"Yes, Thest. I'll be more careful."

3

And so began the education of my vampire child Ilio.

After testing his strength that night, we hunted. Not far from the alder tree, we pounced upon a large buck deer. I took the powerful animal down, wrestling it to the ground by its antlers while Ilio watched. It thrashed and mewled and stamped its hooves.

"Hurry, Ilio, seize it and bite its neck!" I prompted the boy.

"Bite deeply. You must sever the arteries and drink your fill before its heart stops beating."

Eager with hunger, Ilio fell on the beast. He savaged the creature's neck inexpertly, making it squall in pain. The blood flew out the wounds, powered by its galloping heart, and we both ended up soaked before the child had filled his belly.

I broke the creature's neck as a mercy, feeling my own blood hunger yammering in my guts, but my concern was mainly for my vampire child.

How would he feel about this merciless killing? How would he feel about this banquet of blood? Would he be horrified? Disgusted? He was so young, and in many ways, his was a gentler spirit. Yes, he was a child of a hunting society, but the men who'd raised him were protective of him, and I'd been just as sheltering.

Ilio sat back on his knees, wiping his face and then licking the blood from his fingers. He was covered in blood. There was even blood in his curly dark hair, but the look on his face was far from the expression of horror or disgust I'd expected. He grinned in sublime satisfaction, his eyes heavy-lidded. "Oh, that tastes good," he sighed. "Thest, you should drink, too. Aren't you hungry?"

Of course I was hungry for the blood. The smell was maddening. I imagined I could taste it on the air, as if a million tiny droplets of it swirled around my head, but the buck was dead and the blood would be cold and sluggish. The blood of the dead has never been to my liking.

"I will feed later. Dawn is drawing near and we should find a place to sleep, someplace remote where the warriors of the Oombai will not find us."

Ilio turned to the east and saw, as I did, that the horizon was lightening. The rim of the plain was limned with lavender and pink light. The stars there were fading.

We rose. I took a moment to look down at the buck, feeling

pity for the regal animal. It was a lifeless thing now, the night's chill stealing the last of its heat in a faint vapor. Ilio noted the expression on my face and looked confused.

"I know it feels good to feed," I said grimly. "The blood hunger is so overpowering, but it is not seemly to be so callous of the living things that die to sustain our lives. My people gave thanks to the spirits of the beasts who died to feed us when I was a living man, and that is something which I still do."

To my relief, the boy seemed to understand. He nodded gravely. "Then that is what I shall do as well."

"Good. That makes me proud of you, boy."

Ilio smiled, displaying his fearsome new fangs.

I grimaced.

I had many things to teach him.

Taking his shoulder, I said, "Come, let us be rid of these fouled clothes and bathe. I can't stand to be covered in such filth. The smell of all this blood will whip me to madness. When we are clean, we can find some place to rest for the day."

We moved rapidly north, Ilio taking the practice of his new strength quite seriously. I matched my pace to his, feeling no impatience for the boy's weaknesses, only happy to have a companion with which to share these wonders. The guilt I felt at my corruption of him... that I pushed to the back of my mind. That was something I could ponder at length, when we had less compelling business. Tonight we were pressed for time, harried by approaching daylight, hunted by vengeful humans. I had eternity to question my motives and delineate, in fine detail, my offences against this child. Self-accusation and second-guessing could wait. For the time being, it was enough to fly through the air beside him, to cross the plains in great leaps and bounds, taking delight in the trill of his laughter, in his clumsy newborn antics.

We found a shallow creek and shed our clothing, then

glided into the bracing water. I washed the blood and bits of bone and flesh from my skin and Ilio did the same.

"Can we still mate with women, Thest?" Ilio asked as he splashed water in his armpits.

"Yes, of course. Your penis didn't fall off, did it?"

"No!"

I laughed.

"Yes, we can still mate with women," I said more seriously. "But it helps to have a belly full of blood. When you are starved, your flesh will shrivel to your bones, as will your little schtupper. And you must take care not to lose control of your hunger for blood. It will gnaw at you a hundredfold so close to a living human female. You wouldn't want to hurt the woman who's so good as to offer her body to you, now would you?"

Ilio shook his head. "No." But he looked relieved. He'd only just lost his virginity before circumstance—and I, in my weakness—stole his life away.

"Did you not observe me copulating with the female in the village of the Ground Scratchers?" I asked.

Ilio shook his head. He grinned crookedly. "I thought you were just drinking her blood. You… put it in her?"

I groaned and rolled my eyes.

"I wasn't really paying attention!" he laughed.

"Come, boy. Let us set aside such distractions. We need to find someplace to sleep. It is almost daybreak."

I felt suddenly uncomfortable, instructing the boy. In truth, I was but a little more experienced than he was himself. I did not have the right to speak with authority on many of the things he was bound to question me about. I had spent so many millennia in solitude, a hermit in the mountains. Aioa was the first living woman I'd mated with since becoming a vampire. Still, it would do no good to admit my ignorance to the boy. Better that he have confidence in me. He would be less troubled.

As I started away from the creek, Ilio called out. "What about our clothing?"

"Leave them. I'll not wear such filth. The smell of blood on them would drive me mad."

"Oh."

"We'll steal new clothes tomorrow night."

"From who?"

I looked him in the eye. "When night comes tomorrow, I plan to visit my wrath upon the Elders of the Oombai."

He gaped at me, stunned at the ferocious look upon my face.

I spoke no further of my vengeful desires with the boy that night. Instead, I pointed toward a wooded ridge in the distance. "Let us fly that way, Ilio. There is sure to be a cave or some hidden place in that mountainous area where we can rest through the day. I don't know about you, but I'm exhausted. I need sleep."

"So we must rest as we did when we were human?" Ilio questioned.

"Our minds need to dream. Our bodies, I think, could go on without pause, if we cared to push them so far."

For the last time that night, we plied the winds.

On the rocky ridge, we did indeed find a small cavern to curl up in. It was barely large enough for the two of us to wriggle into, but it was high and obscured by brush and thorn bushes and seemed very remote and secure. I fetched a large rock to close the entrance with and pulled it into place behind us. Ilio moved to make room for me and I shifted around in the earthy dark until I'd rooted out a comfortable spot.

There was not much room. I wished we'd had time to find more spacious accommodations, but beggars can't be choosy. Ilio put his head on my shoulder, his fingers twining in the matt of hair upon my chest. I was reminded of my own flesh-and-blood children, how they laid upon me when I was a living man. They'd always plucked at my chest hair the exact same way. I felt a strangling sense of melancholy then, the black and bottomless loss that dogged my every step, as persistent as my thirst for blood. I almost pushed his hand away, but I didn't, because it was good to be a father again… if only a father of deceit.

"Do you love me, Thest?" Ilio asked in the dark.

"Yes, I do," I answered. I did not qualify my reply. I did love the boy.

Ilio snuggled closer to me. "Can I call you 'father'?" he asked.

I winced. Children can always find your vulnerable places!

"Go to sleep, boy," I said in a tight voice.

If my answer hurt him, he did not betray it.

4

My vampire child fell asleep quickly, but I lay awake long into the day. Sunlight glimmered around the edges of the stone I'd used to cover the entrance of the crevice. By its light, I looked at the boy… and looking at the boy, condemned myself.

He was so pale and motionless. In sleep, we vampires give up the pretense of breathing and lie inert. It was horrible to see my child in such death-like repose. He looked, for all intents and purposes, like a frozen white corpse.

I weighed my love for him against my crimes, and came up guilty.

If I lavished him with love the rest of eternity, I could not compensate the boy for the things I'd stolen from him: his family, his innocence, his life. Out of selfishness, I'd made a monster of him, and for that I could never forgive myself.

After a time, he stirred and murmured in his sleep, and for that instant, he looked alive. Wan and unearthly, but alive… but then he fell still again. I had to close my eyes to the travesty. I could not stand to look upon my handiwork any further.

Instead, I contemplated the villains we'd fled from, the men who'd forced me onto this path of death and damnation. Old, wicked and greedy, the elders of the Oombai were worse than any vampires. At least I had the excuse of physical compulsion—the ravening thirst that sometimes drove me to immoral acts. They had no curse compelling them to their behavior, only avarice and evil.

The memory of Aioa's cruel fate kindled my anger further.

I am not a vengeful man, but there must be a reckoning for Ilio's corruption and the murder of the slave woman Aioa. Those Elders had to be taken to task. It was my obligation to mete out their comeuppance, for I was the only one with the power to do it. If I avoided that responsibility, I knew I would forever condemn myself a coward.

Aioa's last words rang in my mind: "I was not born a slave, Blood Drinker. If I had the strength of your kind, I would kill those old men and end the rule of the wicked Oombai, once and for all."

I'd killed their leader Bhulloch, but there remained four others—all just as cruel and greedy as their chieftain.

I recalled their faces in my memory. Tall, imperious Hault. Wizened Y'vort and his nursemaid son Gant, and the fat, hairy boar named Ungst. Callous, grasping men, each one. Slave-keepers. Murderers. Kidnappers of children. For Ilio, I would hunt them down. For Aioa, I would murder them all, and if I could, I would free her sisters and return them to the land they'd been stolen from.

It seemed a noble thing to do. Perhaps, in some small way, I could atone for some of the horrors I myself was responsible for.

Free of their degenerate leaders, perhaps something good would come of the odd tribe of the Ground Scratchers.

Planning my vengeance, I drifted to sleep.

5

Like children are wont to do, Ilio woke before me. I swam to awareness as he wriggled toward the entrance of our burrow. Disoriented and groggy, I watched him push against the stone I'd used to plug the mouth of our warren, realizing just a moment too late that it was still daylight outside our shelter. I opened my mouth to warn him, but my objection rose too slow to my lips. Ilio pushed out the stone before I could stop him and blazing light filled our sleeping hole.

Gleaming gold daggers stabbed into my eyes. Ilio shrieked and fell prone on the earthen floor, clapping his hands over his face.

"My eyes!" he wailed. "Thest, the light--! It hurts!"

Squinting my sensitive eyes to the glare, I slithered around the boy and pulled the stone back into place.

"It's all right now, Ilio," I said, after I'd restored the darkness. I patted him on the shoulder. "You can open your eyes now. It won't hurt."

"Why does the light hurt my eyes so much?" he sniffed.

"The transformation has made your eyes very sensitive. You're a nocturnal creature now."

"But you walk about in daylight."

I smiled. "It doesn't feel very nice."

He regarded me strangely a moment, his eyes rimmed with sticky black tears, and seeing the expression on his face, my guilt made me paranoid. What was he thinking right then? Was he remembering the monster who'd hunted his people in the night, taking one after another until he was the only one left? Had he realized I was the monster who orphaned him?

But no... he was too young. Innocent, he accepted all things at face value—even when the coincidence was too broad.

Perhaps because the coincidence was too broad.

I waited for the horror to dawn in his eyes, the accusations to fly from his lips. But my lies were his truth. He scrubbed his cheeks and smiled.

"I have much to learn," he admitted.

Relieved, I pulled him into my arms and hugged him. "You'll be fine."

We waited until the light shining round the stone first dimmed, then cycled from gold to orange and finally to purple. As we awaited nightfall, we conversed, speaking idly, joking around a little. We talked about the Neirie women Ilio had mated with, then women in general. He wanted to know if I'd ever seen a female Blood Drinker. Mostly Ilio questioned me-- questioned me incessantly, to be honest. He wanted to know about "my people" the Blood Drinkers, what they were like, how I came to be a vampire. I told him of the foul Blood Drinkers who'd plagued my human settlement, and how I'd come, against my will, to be inducted into their ranks, my vampiric sire intending to make me his slave. I told him of my revenge on the brutal being who made me an immortal, and how I'd hid away in the mountains, eschewing human interaction out of fear of harming those I loved.

And that is where my truthful recounting faltered and the lies began. I told Ilio nothing of my attempted suicide, or how I truly came to cross his path. I only told him that, after a time, I decided to come down from the mountains and explore the world, and that I'd crossed his path purely by coincidence, lost in the endless span of the tundra.

"And it was a lucky thing, too," Ilio said. "For there was another Blood Drinker preying on my tribe. A horrible, shriveled thing. If you'd not come along and frightened it off, it probably would have killed me, too."

If I could blush, I probably would have. "Yes. That was a

lucky thing."

"Did you know there was another Blood Drinker hunting on the steppes?"

I shook my head. "No... I sensed no other presence. I was just wandering. I'd lost my way."

"He probably saw you and ran. Perhaps we'll meet him someday," Ilio said. His eyes narrowed with hate. "If we do, I shall try to kill him."

I remained silent.

"It looks as if night has come, Thest," Ilio said.

"Yes, let us rise. We should hunt and continue your training for a while."

As we wriggled from our little cave, Ilio asked, "Are you still returning to the Oombai village?"

I climbed from the hole behind him. The sky was deep blue and sprayed with night's first glittering stars. The temperature was cool and comfortable, a nice breeze rustling the foliage of the surrounding forest. Rising to my feet and dusting off my nude body, I answered the boy.

"Yes. The elders of their tribe have offended me. I do not like how they keep other human beings against their will. I am reminded of the monster that took me captive and forced this transformation upon me. I think it would be a service to their people if I killed the rest of those old men and freed them from their corruption."

Ilio regarded me, his eyes shining with admiration. "I want to go with you."

I laughed. "No, boy. You're too young, and we've not yet completed your training as a Blood Drinker. Your presence would only serve to distract me. I would be too worried about your safety."

Ilio crossed his arms petulantly. Perhaps he thought his stubbornness would impress me, but it only served to illustrate just how young and inexperienced he really was. Yes, he'd matured since our paths crossed. He had a rim of fuzz around his cock and a scruff of hair on his chin, but hairy nuts does not a man make.

Remember, the boy could have been no more than fourteen at the time. In that long ago age, that was nearly a man, but "nearly" was the key word. He was untried, and his face still bore the soft roundness of childhood, with big eyes and a small nose and broad, full lips. He was robust for his age, but he was also short and he had yet to develop a grown man's solidity.

He might one day have made an impressive warrior, but he was trapped now in that place between child and man. It saddened me for him, but there was naught that could be done about it. I had not changed a whit since my transformation to a Blood Drinker, and I did not expect him to mature further—although I could not be certain of it in those days. There was still much I did not know about our vampire nature then.

"Would you have me come to harm, Ilio?" I pressed him, a little exasperated.

"No!" he declared, looking ashamed of himself. "Of course not. Never."

"Then please do not vex me further about this. You nearly died in the village of the Ground Scratchers. I was forced to make you a Blood Drinker to preserve you, or have you forgotten already?"

"No... No. I'm sorry, Thest. I will not defy you."

I sighed. "Don't look so downtrodden, Ilio. It breaks my heart to see it. We will have many adventures together. We have many years ahead of us, and I promise I will not wet-nurse you forever."

He laughed.

Returning his smile, I said, "Now come. I'm starved. Let's find something to eat and we shall practice your new skills for a while before I visit my wrath upon the Oombai."

6

There were deer aplenty in that region, and we fed upon the blood of a young male. This time I let Ilio make the kill. He wrestled the buck to the ground with little difficulty and drank his fill, looking at me with a proud, bloody smile when he was done with it. I finished the beast and we went on our way.

"Tonight," I told him, "We shall practice moving through the tree tops. Observe."

As Ilio watched, I flew naked to the nearest bough and then circled him through the surrounding woodland, a ghost streaking through the branches and rustling leaves. When I leapt down to his side a few minutes later, a couple twigs tangled in my auburn mane, he danced a little in excitement and cried, "Let me try that!"

"Go ahead. Just take care until you've gotten the knack for it. Don't try to impress me. You'll only impale yourself again."

Licking his lips in preparation, the boy flitted into the branches of a nearby tree. He scrambled amid the boughs for a moment, smiled down at me through the greenery, then cut a swathe through the forest in a wide circle. He moved with impressive speed. I think his small stature was an advantage in tree-running. I heard one yelp, and then he flew down beside me, holding his cheek where a branch had slashed his skin.

"How bad did you hurt yourself?" I asked, pulling his hand away.

His injury was already mending. There was a daub of black blood where the branch had gouged him, but that was the extent of it. I watched the lips of the wound draw together and fade.

"I'm fine."

I ruffled his hair. "You did well. That was very fast. I think you must have the spirit of a monkey inside you."

"Thest!" he laughed, but he strutted after that for a little while, high on my praise.

We practiced a little while longer, then I told him I must be on my way if I was to exact my revenge on the Elders and return before daybreak. "I want you to stay near our little burrow tonight. You can make a fire if you'd like, but I forbid you to follow me to that cursed village. If you have any trouble with the humans pursuing us, take to the tree tops and await my return. I don't think they'll find us, but you never know."

"Are you going to kill those old men tonight?" Ilio asked. He had a bloodthirsty look in his eyes.

"Perhaps not tonight. Tonight I shall be the shadow at their doorway. I go to observe and discover their weaknesses. If I have the opportunity, I will take it, but in most instances, Ilio, you will find that caution and wisdom are two sides of the same face. Rest assured, those old men shall pay for their greed and depravity. The Elders remind me of the monster who forced the Blood Curse upon me. It is their avarice that is the root of your untimely transformation. I shall have vengeance for the both of us, and free the Neirie."

"I wish I could join you, Thest," Ilio mused. "I would like to have revenge on them as well." His eyes went very dark as he said it, almost cruel. "I should also like to know what the blood of men tastes like. I suppose it's richer than the blood of animals."

I had no reply to that. The boy spoke the truth.

The German Pornographer Tells All (Part One)

1

"So what happened? Did you kill the last four Elders? And what became of the boy Ilio? Does he still live?"

The German asked these things in a rush. I sat quietly gathering my thoughts, my head down, my white hands clasped between my knees. The curiosity—the need—writ on his features filled me with sadistic pleasure. If my hair were not hanging in my face, he would have seen the enjoyment I took from his curiosity in the twitching of my lips, though I tried to constrain my expressions, lest I betray my weakness to the treacherous man sitting across from me.

You think him helpless, this man sitting bound to my chair with silver duct tape? Men like him are never helpless. They're never anything less than deadly, these human predators. If I were a mortal man, every moment that passed between us would be fraught with danger. He would have taken advantage of any opportunity to free himself. He would have tried to get inside my head. Twist me to his will. Any angle he could think of—bribery, flattery, fear—to suborn my will, confuse me, seduce me, kill me.

Perhaps he already knew my weaknesses.

Yes... I might be immortal, but I have weaknesses.

I'm lonely. I love.

Those are my weaknesses.

Take this man, for instance. My captive. My evening meal. Already, loneliness had stayed my hand. His brutal beauty had enticed me, had led me to bring him here, to my private sanctum, rather than feed on him in some dark corner out there, in the city. I should have made a quick meal of him, tossed the carcass in the Meuse, but I hadn't. And already I was beginning to love him—this killer, this wolf in sheep's clothing. If not love, then fascination. I gazed upon his features, and I imagined how he would appear as an immortal, his flesh white and flawless and gleaming, his grey eyes glittering like diamonds. He would be a God of Death, this man. A terrible angel.

No! Too dangerous to think such thoughts! Was I so desperate for companionship that I would unleash a monster like him on an unsuspecting world?

Ha! I might.

I've done it before.

"I have shared with you," I said quietly. "Now it's time to keep your end of the bargain. I will finish my tale, but first I would have your story."

Lukas licked his lips. His eyes narrowed. Caution. Paranoia. "What do you want to know?" he asked.

I peered at him through the fringe of my bangs. "Start with the girl. The child you raped and murdered tonight. Who was she? How did she come to be in your..." I smiled. "...Not so tender care?"

He stared back at me. I could tell by the tension in his body that he did not want to share his secrets with me. Suspicion comes so easily to men like him. Men with blood on their hands. Paranoia is a country they live their whole lives. Finally, he submitted. He surrendered to my patient stare. His shoulders slumped. "I don't know her name. Not her full name." He sighed. "I don't recall it, anyway. She might have told me once. Yes! Yes, I remember she told me, but I wasn't paying attention. It didn't really matter to me. I only remember her first name. Amelie."

"Amelie," I repeated. A beautiful name. It rolled on the tongue like a candy.

"I came here to Liege to shoot videos for a business associate." He snorted a laugh. "Fuck films, to be precise." For a moment he grinned at me, as if we were partners in his crimes, as if it was all a big joke and we would laugh about it together. "Kiddie porn, to be more precise," he continued. "I'm a child pornographer. I make movies of little kids being raped, and I sell them on the black market." He confessed this as if it were a terrible intimacy. He searched my face for reaction.

I raised one eyebrow. "Is that supposed to shock me? Children have been the victims of monsters like you since the days I walked this earth a living man. The tribe that lived to the north of my people—the Foul Ones-- frequently raided the villages around them for children to exploit. They enslaved them, raped them. They even ate them, and adorned themselves in jewelry made from their bones. Your crimes are nothing extraordinary. You humans eat your young with nauseating regularity, in some manner or other."

He seemed confused for a moment, disconcerted by my lack of outrage.

I was outraged, don't get me wrong. I abhor violence. Man's propensity for visiting suffering on his fellow man sickens me to no end, but in thirty millennia, I have grown inured to any great feelings of surprise or indignation. World-weary. The ultimate cynic. Another weakness, perhaps.

"I apologize," I said with a tiny gesture. "You were saying…?"

His eyes twitched to and fro in their sockets as he searched out the trail of his thoughts, then he said, "I found her at the train station. She'd run away from home with her boyfriend. I didn't care about him. He was just a skinny, blond-headed jono named Bertrand, a dirty keck poseur with an acne-pocked face, but she was something special. Young. Maybe fifteen. Thin and pretty and naive. She was small for her age. She looked much younger than she really was. The two of them were from a little villa in the south. I forgot where they said. Their parents did not approve of their romance, so they bought train tickets and came north to the city. To Liege."

"So there they were, alone, cold, homeless," I prompted.

He laughed. "*Zwei Fliegen mit einer Klappe schlagen.*" Two flies with one swatter!

"And of course, you befriended them."

"It was snowing outside the train station. A beautiful Christmas snow. Flakes as big as your thumbnail. But so cold, and they had nowhere to go. I drove them to my flat. It only took me a few minutes to talk them into my car. I think they knew what they were doing. That they were selling themselves to me for food and shelter. They even saw the cameras and lighting equipment, the bedroom set in the corner of the flat by the windows, but my apartment was warm, and I had lager and reheated some sauerbraten and potato dumplings I had in the refrigerator for them.

"I called Maurice while they were eating. I told him I had some chickens in the coop. He said he'd be right over."

"Maurice?" I asked.

"Maurice Fournier. He's an old friend of my dad. A Frenchman. Or half-French, half-Jew. Something like that. He's a short guy with curly gray hair. Got a big kike nose. He's my financier. He bailed me out of jail when I was arrested in Hamburg. Smuggled me out of the country. Set me up here in Liege under a false identity. I guess you could say he's my producer. He likes the way I shoot my films. Says I alchemize suffering into poetry, or some artsy shit like that. Sometimes he helps shoot and edit my work. Mostly he deals with production, though. Distribution."

I nodded.

"Maurice got there about an hour later. He had Hans with him." Lukas smiled. "Hans Baer. My god, he's a big motherfucker. Almost seven foot tall, with a *wiederschlappen* the size of your forearm. Ugly as sin in the face, big scar running down through his right eye, but the body of an Adonis. If I was a faggot, I would worship that body. It's absolute perfection, from neck to toe. Hans... he stars in a lot of my films. The man can stay hard for hours, and when he cums, it's like someone shook a bottle of champagne and popped the cork." Lukas laughed, blushing a little.

"Hans made my little chicks nervous, with the glass eye and the scar, but they were well on their way to getting plastered, and he has a knack for putting the children at ease. He acts very meek and slouches when he is off camera. Wears hornrim glasses like that American super hero Clark Kent. They're not prescription glasses, though. Just to protect his good eye.

"We all partied for a while. Smoked some hash. Drank. The boy, the skinny jono, wanted to know what all the cameras and lights were for, so I told him. I film young couples for an internet pornsite, I said. He wanted to know how much I paid. When I told him two thousand Euros per shoot, I thought he would shit in his baggies!" Lukas laughed. "You see? I didn't even have to sweet talk them. It no sooner left my mouth than he was begging me to shoot them.

"Of course, she was not so eager, money or no. Young girls protect their virtue like they are setting seed aside for next year's planting, but she was drunk and her boyfriend wouldn't stop badgering her. 'We can get our own place, Amelie!' He said. 'We can live until I find a job to support us!'

"I acted as though I was unsure about it all. I asked them how old they were. Of course, they lied. He told me he was twenty, his girl eighteen. I looked at Maurice and he smiled back at me. It was hard not to laugh.

"Finally, she nodded. She said, 'Yes, all right, Bertrand! I'll do it for us.'"

Lukas's eyes had gone distant. He smiled at the memory.

"So much for love, yes? A few hours in the big city and he was already pimping his girlfriend out. Himself as well. Little whore. The punk wanted their money up front. He thought he was being slick. I counted it out on the table for them to see. Two thousand Euros. And why not? They certainly weren't leaving with it."

2

"She didn't want Maurice and Hans to watch, but I told her I needed them to help with the cameras and lights. I also needed Hans to doll her up.

"The big man was good with makeup and wardrobe. I guess you could say he had an eye for it! Ha-ha! 'We can't shoot you looking like a hobo, now can we?' I asked. So we got her to change into some striped red and white knee highs and a skirt and did her hair up in pigtails. Hans did her makeup and joked around with her until she relaxed. She liked the attention. Hans has a silver tongue. By the time he had her ready for the camera, she was smiling and laughing and looked like her papa's dirty cheerleader fantasy. A little slut with too much makeup and her futz showing through her pink cotton panties.

"Her boyfriend had a rail spike in his baggy pants until he got in front of the camera, then his boner wilted and wouldn't come back. She blew him for a quarter hour while we filmed, but the little prick couldn't get it up. Finally, he said he was going to puke and he pulled his dick out of her mouth and went running to the bathroom.

"I said I'd go check on him. Maurice continued to film her. He was getting some good footage of her licking a giant lolly and playing with herself. Meanwhile, I went to the toilet to check on Juliet's nauseous young Romeo.

"He was on all fours with his head in the crapper when I went in. There was puke all over the floor, puke dripping off the outside of the toilet. He was naked and kneeling in it. I thought of all that good lager and sauerbraten gone to waste and for some reason I got furious. Little boys shouldn't pretend to be men!

"'Are you all right, kid?' I asked, and as I asked I got my knife from my pocket and unfolded it.

"He moaned and puked some more, so I stepped over him from behind and held his head in the pot and stuck the knife in the back of his neck. I shoved it into the base of the skull, the way they'd trained us to do in the military. The punk jerked and slid his knees around in his own puke, but I held his head down and twisted the blade around until he was dead and then I rolled him into the tub and pulled the curtain closed. I flushed his blood and puke down the toilet and washed my knife and my hands and returned to the set.

"Maurice looked at me when I came out and I smiled and shrugged. I showed him the folded knife in my hand, then slid it in my pocket.

"The girl wanted to know if Bertrand was all right. I told her he was fine. But he wasn't going to be able to perform, and he was too embarrassed to come out of the loo right now.

"She wanted to know about the money.

"I shrugged.

"'Maybe… maybe I can do it with one of you,' she said. 'For the money…'

"'Hans has made a few films for us,' I suggested.

"She blinked up at the big man, and I could tell she was scared, but I could tell she was a little bit intrigued, too. He might look like Frankenstein's ugly half-brother, but he'd really charmed her when he was doing her makeup, so she finally nodded, reluctant, and smiled at him. 'Ask... ask Bertrand to stay in the toilet,' she stammered. 'I don't want him to watch me do this.'

"'I'll go talk to him,' Maurice volunteered. He wanted to see what I'd done to the punk. Maurice is the kind of guy who slows down for car accidents. He likes to see all the blood and guts. I think he gets off on it.

"'Is that okay with you?' I asked Hans. Hans smiled, acting all shy and embarrassed, then nodded— just a façade. Just play-acting. It's part of his game. I think the girl, drunk and horny as she was, would have fucked him right then, money or no money. She'd bought his act, hook line and sinker." Lukas flicked his bangs out of his face. "I guess she had a beauty and the beast complex. Probably why she fell for Mr. Pimples.

"'Okay,' I said. 'Camera's still rolling. Amelie, you pretend Hans is your papa, who has caught you being naughty in your bedroom after school. Hans, you will be cross with her until she tries to win your forgiveness with her affection...'

"Maurice returned from the lavatory then. 'He says he's sorry, and he promises to stay in the toilet until it is over,' Maurice tells her. 'He says he loves you too much to watch.' I winced a little at the insincerity in his voice. Mo isn't a very good actor. But lovely little Amelie did not seem to notice. Maurice took his position at camera two, winking at me before ducking his eye to the viewfinder.

"Amelie sniffed with disdain. It was obvious from her expression that Romeo had disappointed her many times in the past. She reclined on the bed and affected a naughty mien, fingers sliding between her thighs. 'Do you want me to lick the lollipop some more?'

"I smiled. 'Whatever you feel inspired to do, my love.'

3

"We shot for three hours straight. Hans is a real animal. I've seen him go for six hours straight, hard as a rail and not one Viagra, but that night, only three. He gets too turned on when they struggle. Especially if they're small and they scream when he puts it in.

"When he climbed onto the bed with her, he dropped the gentle expression from his face like the mask that it was. Poor kid didn't know what hit her.

"Once she caught a look at the python he was packing in his jockey shorts, she tried to beg off, but it was too late for any of that. Her boyfriend was a stiff little keck in my tub and there were no other tenants in the building to hear her cry for help.

"Hans quit playing nice and got down to business. She was willing enough to blow him for a little while, but when he tried to put it in, she started to cry and tried to squirm away from him. She kept crying, 'It's too big! Please! Stop!' Hans finally got tired of wrestling with her. He slapped her hard enough to bloody her nose, then yanked her round little ass in the air and shoved it in to the hilt. Little country bumpkin, she howled like someone lit her futz on fire. He slapped her around some more. Choked her. He took her every way you can imagine, and we got it all on film. When he was finished with her, the chick's face was so purple and swollen her mama wouldn't have recognized her. Hans pumped what looked like a quart of squazzo in her bloody, broken mouth, and then Maurice and I had a go at her.

"You ever have sloppy seconds?" Lukas asked, smiling in a particularly repulsive manner. He licked his lips. "That futz was tenderized! I know most men joke about sloppy seconds, but I find the experience very pleasant. It's softer on the inside. Nice and puffy."

I pretended I did not notice his erection pressing against the zipper of his trousers.

"We bound her with zip ties when we were done with her," he went on. "Taped her mouth real good. We had to get rid of her boyfriend's body. We pulled the shower curtain down and wrapped him up in it, me and Maurice. It's not easy moving a dead body. It's kind of like trying to pick up a sleeping cat. All limp and floppy. It just kind of rolls out of your arms if you're not careful.

"You should have seen the look on her face when we carried him out of the toilet, though, wrapped up in the shower curtain. She knew she was dead too. You could see it in her eyes. The realization. It turned me on so much I told Maurice to hold on and then I walked over to her and rolled her on her side and fucked her again. Just a quickie, but I had to get off. It was just too much of a fucking rush, seeing that look in her eyes.

"'I'm gonna fucking kill you, slut,' I told her as I fucked her. 'You know that, don't you? I'm gonna use you until I've used you all up, and then I'm gonna kill you, just like I killed your fucking boyfriend.' I had her mouth taped up so she couldn't scream, but I could see her face. I could see the tears running down her cheeks, and I blew another load in her swollen little snatch while I watched her cry. Her bleeding little reamed out snatch…"

I watched the German's face as he recounted the incident, the flush of arousal in his cheeks, the sheen of perspiration on his brow and upper lip. My hunger leapt inside me and I had to hold myself immobile, lest I seize him and drain him right that instant. I have preyed on the wicked for millennia. The sight of such unrepentant evil stirs my hunger to unbearable heights.

No! I told myself. *Not yet!* There is still much you desire from this fiend! I wanted his life. His whole life. I wanted to hear him recount his evils. His confessions were like seasoning. They would make my meal, when I surrendered to my appetite, all the more delicious.

I restrained myself, but barely, and speaking in a husky rasp myself, I urged him on.

"So what did you do with the boy?" I asked.

He blinked. Looked at me as if he'd forgotten I was sitting there listening. "The jono? Oh… we, uh… took him to the pier. No one ever goes down to those wharves anymore. We drove down there with the kid in my trunk. Took him out and tossed him in the Meuse. We, uh… pulled some of his teeth and cut off his hands first, so it would be difficult to identify the body. On our way back to my flat, we took a little detour through the ghetto and threw his hands and teeth down a storm drain. Let the rats have them."

"And the girl? How long did you keep her?"

"About a week."

4

He went on to describe, in graphic detail, the ruination of Amelie.

Lukas and his cohorts continued to abuse and molest the child until all that remained was an inhuman thing, starved, mute, the hopeful young girl she once was consigned to drift like a ghost inside her own mind, howling inside the haunted house that was her skull. When she was used up, they called over a gentleman named Huang Zhiyua, who they intended to sell the remains to, but Mr. Zhiyua took only a brief perusal of the merchandise before walking away, holding his nose and flapping his hand in her direction. There was nothing left to do but dispose of the body then-- still living, yes, but little more than animate flesh.

Lukas left his flat at midnight—less than five hours ago—walking the girl onto the icy streets wrapped in nothing but a threadbare blanket. He'd raped her one last time before he decided it was time, and his semen still trickled down her thighs as she stumbled to his car like a zombie. When he opened the trunk and gestured for her to get in, Amelie climbed obediently inside.

She didn't fight. She didn't cry for help. She welcomed death. For her, it would be a relief, I'm sure. An end to hunger. An end to thirst. An end to shame and degradation.

This man, my captive, had just snapped her neck and tossed her into the Meuse when I spied him from my perch on an abandoned warehouse. When I flashed down from the snowy sky and snatched him from the ground, the impact knocked him unconscious. If I had not seen him murder such a beautiful child, and if he were not so beautiful himself, I probably would have killed him right there. Drained his blood on the roof of the abandoned warehouse and then flung his remains into the icy river with the body of the child. Instead, I was beguiled, and, despite my hunger, I wanted to know him, and I wanted to know the child he'd murdered so heartlessly. So I brought him to my home, leaving his car running on the pier. Leaving the child's steaming puddle of urine to freeze upon the grease-stained wharf.

When he had finished speaking, Lukas pulled a face and asked, "You have something to drink, Drac? My mouth is dry."

I rose without answering and walked into the kitchen to pour him a glass of water.

As I went, I curled forward a little, putting my hand upon my belly. My blood hunger was twisting me up inside. The pain was horrid, a wrenching, burning sensation in my guts. I did not know how much longer I could resist it before I was forced to consummate this brief affair.

Oh, what a mess it was going to make! When I'm this hungry, I'm a savage. He'll probably be torn to pieces!

Unless…

As I filled a glass with water, my mind seized upon an alternate plan. Something that would buy me a little more time with this beautiful villain. I grinned as it came into my thoughts, full blown and wonderful.

It would be apt, the justice of it both beautiful and brilliant.

As I returned to the bedroom, Lukas eyed me nervously. "I don't like the way you're looking at me, Count," he said as I approached him.

I smiled. I didn't bother to hide my fangs. "You shouldn't."

I held the glass to his lips and allowed him to drink. As his Adam's apple bobbed, I stared at the veins in his neck and temple, throbbing almost imperceptibly beneath his flesh. My free hand wandered toward his throat and I jerked it back to my side.

He gasped when I took the glass away. I turned to set it on my dresser and he belched softly and excused himself.

"We have a little problem, you and I," I told him.

"How's that?"

"I don't believe I can resist killing you much longer," I said.

He stared at me without expression. "That sucks," he replied.

I laughed softly as I sat back down on the edge of my bed. "I have a proposition for you. Something that may allow me to converse with you a little longer."

"And what's that?" he asked suspiciously.

"I want you to call your friend Hans. I have a cell phone. I will dial his number for you. You will call him and invite him here to my home. I will give you the address. Tell him... Oh, I don't know." I waved my hand absently. "Tell him you met some lovely young women, but there are two of them, and they'd like him to come over and join the party. Tell him whatever you think will convince him to come."

"You're planning to kill him and drink his blood so we can talk a little while longer," Lukas said. The viciousness of my proposal made him grin. There was a look, too, of fascination on his face, as if I'd promised him a magic show.

I rose and drifted toward the balcony doors. "Of course."

"Maybe I don't want to talk anymore. Maybe I'd rather just get it over with," he suggested.

"Do you really want to die right now?" I asked, turning suddenly toward him.

He took in my gleaming gold eyes, my white shriveled flesh and long, curved fangs, and thought better of it. Shaking his head, he stammered, "N-no. I guess not. I'll call him."

"I thought as much."

Lukas squinted at me. "He's a big fucker," he said.

I walked to the fireplace and picked up one of the pokers. Smiling mildly, I bent it into a U shape. I flexed it, then snapped it in two and tossed the pieces on the floor with a clatter.

"Fuck," he wheezed.

"I'll go get my cell phone," I told him, striding across the floor.

He stopped me as I reached the doorknob. "I'll do it, but I have one condition," he called out to me suddenly, speaking in a rush.

I put my hand on the doorframe. I didn't look at him. "And what would that be?" I asked.

"I want to watch you do it," he whispered behind me.

I smiled, but it was not a smile of amusement. It was a

smile of despair. "Of course," I murmured. "If that's what you'd like."

5

Lukas made the call, or rather, I made the call for him. I dialed the numbers as he ran them off for me, tapping the keyboard of my modern little phone with my long, white finger. I was unsure as I held my cell phone to his lips if he would actually betray his friend, or if he would dare to warn him off-- maybe even plead to the man for assistance-- but he did pretty much what I asked of him, and I have to give him credit: he's a very persuasive fellow. Despite the hour, he enticed and cajoled Hans until he'd convinced the man to get up, throw some sexy duds on, and drive across town to my suite. My prisoner looked up at me with a strange mixture of fear and hate and excitement when I snapped the phone shut and ended the call.

"He's coming," he said. "He'll be here in thirty minutes."

I left the room without speaking. As I neared the door, the pornographer called out behind me: "Remember what you promised!"

I closed the door and crossed my apartment to my dressing room. There, I tied back my hair and applied cosmetics to my hands and face and throat so that I would appear, at least for a few moments, like a living man. The flesh-colored foundation, manufactured by a company called Lancome, concealed the pallor of my flesh and the wriggling blue worms of my blood-starved veins. Except for the eyes, I looked... almost human.

The eyes would give it away, but I only needed the man to step inside. He would not notice the strange gleam of my stare. Not until I'd closed the door and locked it behind him. Then it would not matter.

As a final bit of preparation, I set the stage for the second act of this evening's performance. I put a CD in my stereo system and turned the volume up loud, then mussed up my living room, pulling a couple pillows askew on my sofa. I surveyed the room, my hands on my hips, then grabbed a pair of my trousers and tossed them on the floor.

Smiling at my handiwork, I recalled a line from the old children's poem:

"Will you walk into my parlor?" said the Spider to the Fly...

I waited patiently near the door, my appetite increasing with every passing moment. The hunger inside me was a fire sizzling in my guts, burning inside every wriggling vein. Thirty minutes passed. Then forty. Lukas called from my bedchamber: "Is he here yet?" and I commanded him to be silent. Forty-five minutes after my captive had convinced his associate to come and party with us, I heard the elevator down the hallway *ding!* The doors slid open and footsteps trod toward my apartment. Heavy footfalls. A big man.

I could smell him as he drew near. Too much cologne. Cigarettes on his fingertips and lips. I could smell the leather jacket he wore. The mints in his pocket. The odor of his flesh. His sexual excitement (Lukas had told him there were women waiting, young and drunk and willing, looking for a fourth).

The doorbell chimed. I waited. On the second ring, I opened the door.

"Hello?" I said.

Lukas was not exaggerating. Hans was a huge man. Almost seven foot tall, and powerfully built. He was dressed in a leather jacket and white silk shirt, open to the breastbone to expose his sculpted pectorals and a large gold crucifix.

(Don't worry, my readers. As you'll recall, religious icons have no effect on me!)

His horn rim glasses were fogged from the cold outside.

The Oldest Living Vampire on the Prowl

His lank blond hair—so pale it was almost white—hung down in a stylish shag from beneath a toboggan speckled with melting snowflakes. His nose was red from the cold, and he was sporting American blue jeans so tight the full length of his cock could be seen running several inches down his pants leg.

What is the motto?

Ah, yes! If you've got it, flaunt it.

The large man looked down at me with surprise, then his one good eye narrowed with suspicion. "Who are you?" he asked. He had to yell to speak over the pulsing music.

I told him I was the Diener... the butler.

"Please, come in," I said, standing aside and sweeping my arm out.

He walked in, scanned the room as he slipped off his jacket. "Is Mr. Jaeger still here?" he asked. The puckered scar on his face was deep. I wonder how he'd gotten it. His glass eye didn't quite align with the eye that was still sighted. It peered off at a disconcerting angle, rimmed with a bit of mucous.

"The group has retired to the bedroom," I said with just a hint of feigned disdain. He tossed his leather jacket into my arms and I folded it and draped it upon a settee. I shut the door, locked it, threw the deadbolt. After a moment of consideration, I chained it, too.

"Where?" he yelled.

I turned and gestured toward the door across the room.

"Lukas?" he called, as he plodded toward the bedroom. "Hey! Don't start the party without me!"

I stalked quietly behind him. The scent of his blood was maddening. I inhaled the smell as it billowed around me in his wake, hot and salty and nourishing.

Hans opened the door.

Lukas ogled him, bound to my Louis the Fifteenth with silver duct tape.

"What the fuck?" the giant exclaimed.

Even for his bulk, the big man was quick. He spun around as I lunged at him. His fist shot out like a cannon, but for all his speed, I was faster. He might as well have been moving in slow motion.

I pivoted, arched back. His strike pierced only air.

Hans stumbled forward into my arms, and I swung him around and onto my bed. His eyewear clattered on the floor. We collapsed upon my sheets like lovers. I looked at Lukas for a second, saw him watching with wide eyes and a stunned—but rapt—expression, then I curled my lips back from my fangs and sank my teeth into the big man's neck.

Hans howled in agony. He tried to push me away, but I was too powerful for him. I was snarling. The world went red and hazy as I fed. The pleasure was orgasmic. I gripped his blond hair and jerked his head sideways. I heard his vertebrae crunch. I nearly pulled his head completely off, but I was beyond care. I was beyond reason, beyond mercy. Well beyond good manners! I was so hungry, and the blood was so hot and tasty… and there was so much of it! This giant was a veritable smorgasbord. An all you can eat buffet of blood!

My chin was dripping. My sheets and mattress, I'm sure, were ruined.

He was dead, but I was still hungry.

I tore his shirt open and plunged my fist into his sternum, punching through flesh and bone. I pried open his ribs, ripped out his heart and squeezed it into my mouth. I lapped at the blood that drizzled from his entrails, then finally, thinking of all the runaways and kidnapped children he had raped and murdered, I shucked down his jeans—despite the cold, he was wearing no underwear—and I tore his cock and balls from between his quivering legs.

I wheeled toward my captive, holding the man's organs in my bloody fist.

Lukas was watching in horror... but he was also aroused. I could smell his sexual excitement. I could see the evidence of it pressing the front of his slacks out.

"You covet this?" I demanded, the rapist's penis flopping in my fist. "This is what you serve? This is your god?" Not meaning Hans's penis specifically, but The Penis. Lust, and its gratification.

Lukas shook his head no.

I flashed toward him, moving faster than he could see. As the speed of my movement blew back his expensively styled bangs, I grabbed him by the hair and forced the mutilated genitals into his mouth... as much as would fit in there. They really were quite enormous!

"The Catholics eat the flesh of their god. You can do the same!" I hissed. I was enraged, trembling. I turned brusquely away, tried to reign in my emotions.

Lukas spat the torn and shriveled cock from his mouth and screamed. It was an outraged, womanish cry. His face and clothes were smeared with his associate's blood. "You bastard!" he howled. "You fucking monster!" He retched, then vomited into his own lap.

My back still turned to him, I started laughing. "Yes, that's right. I am a monster! What did you think you were dealing with?"

He puked again, then groaned, dry heaved a couple more times. He raised his head, his eyes bleary, snot hanging from his nose. He began to thrash against his bonds. Hysteria had taken his reason. He wrenched back and forth in the chair, making it hop and scoot on the floor.

I turned and struck him with my foot. The blow drove him across the room, chair and all, and he crashed against the wall.

The impact shattered my expensive antique chair.

Oh, now that was a waste! That chair was 300 years old!

Lukas lay crumpled and unconscious on his side, plaster

dust drifting from the chipped drywall above.

I sighed, disappointed with my loss of control. After a moment, I walked to the pornographer and checked to see if he still lived.

6

"I'm going to kill you," I said when he opened his eyes. "Have no doubt of that. My question to you is this: do you want to hear the rest of my story before I do it?"

The Battle with the Elders

1

The thought of sinking my fangs in the necks of those old villains stirred me to passion. I left the boy with a stern admonition to keep out of trouble, then I took to the tree tops and flew through the boughs and branches down the side of the low mountain. I paused near the border of the plains and scampered to the top of a towering spruce, clinging to the swaying trunk to look out across the undulating green landscape. Very far away, the orange light of a couple campfires glimmered on the plains: the warriors the Elders had sent after us. But the warrior camp was kilometers away. They could never hope to cross the distance to our hiding place in the rugged hills before I returned, even if they knew which direction to travel, which I'm sure they didn't.

I toyed with the idea of descending upon them. Without the boy to look after, I would make short work of them, and I'd fed very little before setting off on my mission. It might be enjoyable to take a couple of them for my dinner, send the rest of them fleeing in terror… but my heart shied away from the needless cruelty. The offense did not lie with the huntsmen; it resided with their masters.

Pushing aside my brief fantasy, I took a better grip of the spruce and leaned back, causing the top of the tree to bend earthward. As it rebound, I used the forward momentum to give my leap a little extra *oomph*. I stretched out like a bird in flight, my arms spread to my sides for a moment, before I twisted around in midair and descended into the emerald canopy below.

I weaved my way through the limbs and foliage, climbing, swinging, leaping from branch to branch. When the forest thinned, I dropped to the ground and sprinted across the grassy plains, pumping my arms and legs at full speed.

Every now and then I look a mighty leap to get a broader view of my surroundings. I made better speed when I stayed earthbound, but it just wasn't as fun.

As I drew near the country of the Ground Scratchers, I slowed my advance.

I flitted past the few scarce huts sprinkled along the perimeter of the strange tribe's territory, those peculiar dwellings made of sticks and grass and stone. I could smell the bodies of the inhabitants sleeping inside, unwashed men and women, curled up with their children for the night. Some of the homes were surrounded by patches of exposed earth with food plants growing in rows within the borders. Other huts were adjacent to enclosures imprisoning sleeping animals: reindeer and more of those great, feathered beasts we'd seen the day we first entered the country of the Ground Scratchers. The gargantuan birds hunkered in dug out depressions in the dirt with their heads tucked under their wings, an outlandish scene.

The sight of the enslaved animals disturbed me. My people were hunter-gatherers, and though my tribe had lived off the bounty of the land, we were children of nature. We had no delusions of its mastery. We did not try to enclose it or possess it... or our fellow man.

These Ground Scratchers are grasping fools, I thought. What kind of madmen think they can possess the world?

Or perhaps I was the fool, and time had moved on without me.

My passage went unobserved. My silent movements did not even rouse the dogs.

I rounded the hill and looked down upon their primitive little city, impressed again by its breadth and the multitude of dwellings therein. The moon gleamed on the surface of the winding river beyond. Torches gleamed and flickered, so many it looked like the stars had fallen into the avenues of the village.

The task of finding the elders among all these homes suddenly seemed daunting. How could I find the old degenerates in this vast settlement without roaming from hut to hut? I was fast and silent, but eventually some sentry or servant would spy my movements, and then I would have to flee once again.

Then I thought of Aioa—beautiful, fiery Aioa—and I thought of Ilio-- his innocence lost forever-- and I gathered my resolve.

Holding my anger close to my heart, I descended unto the village of the Oombai.

2

Aioa's face floated in my mind as I slipped through the dark avenues. I kept seeing her eyes-- the way they bulged from their sockets when Bhulloch's servant yanked her head back and cut her throat. The shock and betrayal in them. I'd asked for her freedom in return for my assistance, but the Chief Elder had misunderstood. The chieftain thought I was literally asking for her life ... and bent eagerly to the task. She thought I was a willing accomplice. That I'd called for her sacrifice. Her final horror-struck expression was etched forever in my immortal memory now.

I moved through the thoroughfares, slipping from shadow to shadow—an outlandish sight, I'm sure. A tall naked savage, white skin glowing in the moonbeams, moving too fast, too lightly to be human. My eyes engulfed the eldritch light, amber coals in the black hollows beneath my brow.

I avoided the dancing glow of the torches. When sentries passed my way, I slipped silently around the corner of a hut, or ducked behind a tree or bush or low stone wall.

Most of the village's denizens were sleeping, but here and there a lodge was lively. I peeked through a crack in the wall and watched slave women dancing for a group of swaying drunkards. I spied on revelers and love-makers and gamblers. In one large hut, naked men covered in lard were wrestling inside a ring as others cheered them on. In another, a brutal man was whipping the naked back of an emaciated servant.

The servant cowered and begged for mercy, crying out each time the lash fell. His back was striped and bloody, but his pleading won him no respite.

This culture thoroughly confused and disgusted me. I could not fathom its dynamics. Why did the slaves not rise up against their brutal masters? Why did this bloodied servant not take a weapon and put it in his master's belly? There were plenty of them at hand.

And I still had not found the lairs of the elders.

Frustrated, I paused to gather my thoughts. Squatting beside a shrub, I asked myself: Where would such men place their dwellings? It would be in a central location—one that afforded both comfort and security. The Elders would vie for prominence, esteem. They would own grand lodges. Dwellings large enough to house their servants, to secret their ill-gotten possessions, to lord their position of power over the other inhabitants of this country.

The central plaza, of course. Somewhere near there.

I rose and scuttled toward the center of the village. The concentric stone walls of the courtyard come into view, deserted at this hour of the night. Beyond that, perched upon a low prominence were several broad and well-maintained huts.

They were too large to be called huts, actually. They were, in size, more similar to the halls of the Viking people, a true miracle of modern architecture by the standards of that primitive era. Three broad lodgings, crowded close together, built of timber and thatch and stone, and decorated with hanging plants and great mammoth tusks that were inscribed with ornate imagery.

They were guarded, of course. A quartet of grim-looking men stood watch at the perimeter of the elders' lodges, armed with spears.

I circled around, staying in the shadows, moving in a low-to-the-ground crouch. I slipped behind a tree, then flitted behind the timber posts of another animal enclosure.

But no--! This was no animal enclosure. I smelled human blood, human sweat, the high rich stink of human excrement. Rising a little, I peered toward the far end of the pen and saw a small group of slaves, huddled together beneath a primitive lean-to, wrapped in stinking hides.

The sight of the emaciated humans fueled my anger. My mind flashed on the image of Neanderthals, lying stiff and dead in my maker's charnel pit. My lips split back from my fangs in furious indignation.

One of the sentries had wandered a little too far into the shadows. He was leaning on the shaft of his spear, his back to me, preparing perhaps to steal a little nap.

When I saw the opportunity, I struck.

I blurred through the unlit rear grounds, coming up behind the delinquent guard and clapping my palm across his mouth. Before he could react, I curled the fingers of my other hand into his neck and pulled out his throat.

I dragged him further around the corner so that his corpse would be well out of sight and lowered his still twitching body to the ground. Taking a moment to lick my bloodied fingers– I couldn't help myself, it smelled so good!—I slipped quietly toward an opening in the wall of one of the Elder lodges. As silent as a spirit, I peeked inside, pushing the plaited hanging to the side with my fingers.

The dwelling was impressively large, with a multitude of furs and low, simple furnishings sprawled across the oiled dirt floor. Many of the room's occupants were sleeping, but there was an old man sitting near the fire, smoking a long and ornately carved pipe. The wizened elder named Y'vort. He was rocking slightly, humming a song under his breath.

I cast my gaze about the room and saw the ancient man's nursemaid, his son, sleeping on a nearby mat. Elder Gant.

I knew it would be a simple thing to slip inside the lodge and dispatch the two men, but I withdrew, allowing the hanging to drop back into place. Sneaking through the dark to the next hut, I peeked through a chink in the wall and spied the elder Ungst mating with a slave girl, his fat bearded face twisted with pleasure. He was thrusting against her brutally, his fingers digging into the flesh of her hips, making her cry out in pain.

The elder Hault must reside in the next dwelling, which was the largest of the three. I wondered where Bhulloch had slept. Maybe with the other two, Y'vort and his son. They were the eldest of the five.

As I started toward Hault's lodge, however, a cry of alarm rose in the night: a man's exclamation of surprise. I twisted around and saw one of the sentries blinking down at his dead fellow's corpse. Before the guard could raise his eyes and find me in the shadows, I leapt toward the bough of a nearby tree. I vanished among the foliage with hardly a rustle and watched as the other sentries came running.

The Oldest Living Vampire on the Prowl

A few seconds later, half a dozen armed men came stumbling from Hault's lodge, babbling and brandishing spears and knives. Elder Hault strode from his dwelling, pulling his cloak about his shoulders. He snapped orders at the disorganized mob in an imperious tone.

The armed men fanned out and began to search for me.

So they were expecting me, I thought. Or they feared my retribution. I wasn't surprised.

I watched as the elder Y'vort tottered out and conferred with Hault. They spoke together in low voices. I craned forward to listen. I was beginning to grasp the language of the Oombai. The sounds had begun to congeal into meaning.

"*Fallehn t'horn*-- Blood Drinker—*e'ei hobphen*—tonight!" Hault murmured, his eyes flicking this way and that as he spoke, betraying his nervousness.

Y'vort nodded. "Yes! Yes! *T'horn e'ei hemm trod ei'skii!* I told you as much."

Suddenly, the Elders jerked their heads in my direction, their bodies stiffening with alarm. For a moment, I saw their eyes drink in the torchlight. Their pupils shone, a dim orange glow.

I froze a little in shock.

The blood they traded for with my vampire brethren--! They must have drunk enough of it to alter them physically! Their senses were sharper than a normal human's senses. I wasn't expecting that.

As they howled for their guards, their gnarled fingers waving in my direction, I launched myself from the tree at them, snarling like a sabre-tooth cat. The tall elder named Hault threw himself to the ground with surprising speed, but ancient Y'vort was not so quick.

I landed a few feet away and seized the old man's head in my hands.

"Call upon your goddess to save you now!" I challenged

him.

As he mewled in terror, I twisted his head violently to the side. The moist crunch of bone within the wattled flesh of his neck gave me a thrill of satisfaction.

I let the wrinkled body crumple to my feet.

I expected the old man to be dead when he hit the earth, but the vampire blood he had drunk through the years had fortified him. Not enough to preserve his life. He didn't heal.

For a time he lay twitching on the ground, his head twisted round in an unnatural position, his eyes glaring up at me, filled with hatred and pain. I was momentarily distracted by the grotesque sight. I pulled my gaze away finally, turned to kill Hault, but before I could move to seize him, a spear whooshed through the air toward me, and I was forced to contort my body backwards to elude it.

"Kill it! Kill it!" Hault wailed, lying prone on the ground with his arms covering his head.

The starved men and women in the slave pen were stirring. I heard their frightened murmurs, saw a couple of them peek through the fence rails at the nearby chaos. I wondered if any of them were Aioa's sisters, but I couldn't tell, not by just the eyes.

A dozen warriors were running my direction, streaming from all quarters. Two more spears left their hands and whistled toward me.

I launched myself into the air to avoid them. Landing on the thatched roof of Y'vort's lodge, I ran to the far end—stumbling as the roof sagged beneath my bare feet—and then I leapt toward the central plaza.

I landed in a crouch, looked over my shoulder to make sure there were no projectiles flying toward me from the rear, then I ran.

I'd lost the element of surprise—a minor setback, by my reckoning. Of my enemies, only three remained.

And I would return with the dark to kill them.

Tomorrow night, I promised them silently.

3

"Thest! You're all right!" Ilio exclaimed. He was sitting cross-legged by the fire he'd made, waiting for me in the clearing outside the entrance of our warren. He flew to his feet to welcome me, relief etched in his features.

"Of course I'm all right," I smiled at him. "Did you think otherwise?"

He shrugged, embarrassed. "Who can know the future?" he asked. "I only know I do not want to be an orphan again."

I hugged him and promised, "I will not let that happen."

"Come sit with me. Tell me what happened," he said anxiously.

We sat near the crackling fire. He'd made a good one in my absence. It could probably be seen by the warriors who pursued us on the plains, blazing as it did on the side of the mountain, but I was not worried about them. They were far across the grasslands and had not moved much nearer when I'd checked from the treetops on my return. I relaxed and watched the flames. The logs popped and hissed as the blue and orange tongues lapped over them. I could feel its heat tighten the surface of my cold, white flesh. It felt good.

The boy looked ethereal in the orange glow of the leaping flames, his skin smooth and shimmering. His curiosity was plain to see in those glittering blue eyes, so plain it almost made me laugh.

"Did you find us some clothes?" Ilio asked.

I shook my head. "Unfortunately, no. I was forced to retreat from the Oombai village. The Elders have a secret which caught me by surprise."

"What is that?"

I quickly recounted my adventure. Ilio's eyes grew wide as I told him the effect our brethren's blood had wrought on the old men I'd sworn vengeance against. When I finished my tale, he said, "We should leave this country, Thest. Who cares what these people do? They're all mad!"

Thinking of Aioa's accusing last glare, seeing the boy's white lifeless flesh, my countenance darkened with indignation. "I care, boy. Those old men have offended me. They have offended us both. They're wicked and they must be brought to task."

Ilio recoiled from my angry tone. "I'm sorry, Thest. I only worry for your safety. We are strong, but I know we can die. I see it in your eyes when you look at me. Your fear for me."

I sighed. "Don't apologize, Ilio. Your counsel is wise." I looked to the south, toward the country of the Ground Scratchers, then chuckled, turning back to him. "You remind me of an old companion. I rarely took his advice either. It was a habit that often got me in trouble."

"So we will leave this country?" he asked hopefully.

"Yes," I answered. "Tomorrow night, I will return and kill those old men, and then we will leave."

Ilio grinned, rueful at my stubbornness. "Then come and rest, father," he said, rising. "You need to be refreshed when you return to your war."

I did not reproach him for calling me "father", though it troubled me. I rose and followed him into our earthen burrow. The sky was lightening, the horizon aflame. There were thick clouds drifting in from the north, promising rain. Ilio scurried in before me, then I squatted down and slid inside too. I closed our hole to the coming light and curled up next to my adopted child to rest, and though I thought my sleep would be slow in coming, my mind drifted away quickly.

I dreamed that morning.

The Oldest Living Vampire on the Prowl

I dreamed of the fiend who made me a vampire. I dreamed of the charnel pit and the mounds of dead Neanderthals therein. That pit was where he held me captive, where he stole away my humanity. In my dream, I was a man, and I was clawing at the slick stone walls, trying to climb, trying to escape the cavern full of cold, stiff corpses, but every time I managed to ascend a meter or two, the slippery limestone crumbled under my fingers and I fell back onto the lifeless, savaged bodies of his victims. I railed at the moon peeking through the entrance of the pit, frustrated and afraid. My terror felt real in my dream. Although the event had transpired in the far distant past, my dream that morning had an immediacy that convinced my sleeping mind that it was real, it was all real, and it was happening right now.

I rose to try the wall again, and that's when his shadow fell across me.

The monster, my maker, dropped silently from the entrance of the charnel pit, his fur cloak spreading out like the wings of a great carrion bird. There was no place in the gourd-shaped pit to run or hide. I could only throw my back against the slick wall and squeeze my eyes shut. I slid down until I was sitting on the gruesome floor of the cavern. It was only when I heard no other sound from the monster that I dared to peek out.

My maker was gone. In his stead, the Elders of the Oombai glowered.

The five old men stood in a semi-circle around me, their bodies bent and leathered by time. Bhulloch, Y'Vort, Gant, Ungst and Hault—all glared down at me with furious contempt. At their feet lay the bloodless corpse of my adopted son Ilio, his flesh white as snow, his eyes empty of all but a lingering expression of pain. The faces of the old men were masks of spiteful pleasure, and in each of their eyes, drowned in pools of black shadow, was a tiny, glowing moon, moist and silvery. Those terrible eyes were angled down at the corpse of my child, but as I sat shivering just a few feet away, they twitched in my direction, and I was frozen to my soul at the terrible hunger in them.

I feared, not for what they were, but for what they might become.

4

I awoke with the thought that I should arm myself. I could not know the extent of the remaining elders' powers, and it would be foolish to attack them and their army without weapons and armor of my own. It was unwise to venture into their village last night, so naked and unprepared. I knew the limits of my own transformed body, but what tricks might those wily old monsters possess? What if they managed to restrain me? Could they drain me of my Living Blood somehow? Steal the source of my immortality?

I'd grown overconfident of my strength.

Tonight I must be prepared.

Thinking this, I turned my body over in our little earthen burrow and realized our retreat was slick and cold with mud. It had rained while we slept and water had seeped inside. A puddle had formed at the bottom, several inches deep. My feet were lying in the pool to my ankles.

The boy lay at my side in death-like repose, his black hair curling at his pale brow, his chest unmoving. It was always disconcerting to see him sleeping so still. Even his heart was silent, beating only once every few minutes, and weakly at that. It is the Strix which preserves us, not our human organs.

And what of this child? I thought to myself. Was I being a fool on his behalf? Might it not be a disservice to him to protect him so jealously from harm? What would become of him, sheltered and untrained in war, if something should happen to

The Oldest Living Vampire on the Prowl

me? He would be weak and defenseless. He did not have my strength and invulnerability to rely on. The dark blood had worked a lesser miracle on his flesh. In strength, he was only slightly more powerful than the little pet my maker had kept, the strange and twisted Blood Drinker I had killed with a blow to the breast, the one we'd called the Lizard Man.

"Ilio, wake up. It is night," I said, nudging the boy.

Ilio's blue-white eyelids fluttered open and his face and flesh took on the animation of life. He turned his head to me and smiled, then became aware of the muck we wallowed in. His lips twisted into a grimace. "Yuck!" he exclaimed, holding his dripping hands before his eyes.

"It rained," I said, then rolled over and crawled toward the entrance of the small cavern. The mud squished and bubbled between my fingers as I slithered forward on my hands and knees. I pushed the stone out of the opening and clambered out onto the mountainside.

The sky overhead, I saw, was thick with clouds, but for the time being it was not raining. There was a flicker of lightning in the lowering heavens, a series of low, pulsing strobes. Thunder rumbled in the distance.

The forest surrounding us was slick and dripping, its denizens hushed by the recent downpour. The atmosphere was heavy and seemed charged with the promise of another violent deluge.

Ilio climbed out behind me and stood waiting. His white flesh was smeared with mud.

"Let us find a pool to bathe in," I said, and he nodded. Looking over my shoulder at him, I smiled and said, "See if you can keep up with me, little monkey."

I leapt into the bough of the nearest tree and flew through the forest toward a fall I had come across. I heard Ilio pursue me, laughing as he tried his best to keep up with me. It was a game, but in truth I was testing him as well, taking a measure of his speed and strength. I was quite pleased to find that he had little trouble moving through the treetops, and if he were just a bit stronger and faster, he might have actually overtaken me.

The woodland ended abruptly ahead. It seemed the world had come to an edge and there was only sky beyond. I dived into the empty air. Below me, the roar of white water, cascading over a rocky escarpment. I fell toward the foaming pools. Fizzing liquid enveloped me.

I surfaced, swept my wet hair from my eyes, looked up just in time to see Ilio dropping over the cliff behind me, his arms and legs pumping. I jumped out of the way as he disappeared in the spume, a great explosion of water blooming up in the fuming mist.

He burst from the water, laughing. "I almost caught up with you!" he boasted.

"You did very well," I agreed.

Grinning, he dunked his head in the water and scrubbed the mud from his hair. I did the same, and when I could not wash it all out, the boy waded to me and helped. He squeezed the clinging mud from my wavy locks, swirled my hair in the churning water.

"I wish my hair was long like yours," he said wistfully. He used his palms to wipe the last of the mud from my shoulders. "It does not grow after becoming what we are, does it?"

"No."

I swam toward the shore, my body gleaming and white again. Climbing onto the mossy rocks, I waited for Ilio to join me.

The boy had paused, hip-deep in the pool. He was looking down at his hands, his face thoughtful. I spoke before he could voice the realization in his eyes:

"You are strong, but the dark blood has left you far too vulnerable for my comfort. If you are brave, I would like to try to strengthen you. I have been remiss in my responsibilities toward you. I should not shelter you so much. You should know how to defend yourself in battle. You should know how to fight, and if necessary, how to take men for your sustenance. My only excuse is that I love you, and I wished to preserve your innocence a while longer."

Ilio nodded gravely. "I understand, fa—I mean, Thest."

I smiled. "In many ways, I have become your father, Ilio. I gave birth to this cold life you now have. I would rather you consider me a brother, however. It will strengthen you to think of yourself a man, not a man's son."

"And how will you try to make me a stronger Blood Drinker, Thest?"

"You were dying when I made you as you are, so you do not remember, but the trick is a simple one. I must pass the Living Blood inside me into your body. This was how I was made this cold white thing many years ago, and this is what I did to you."

"And you wish to do it again? To see if it will make me hardier?"

I nodded.

Ilio drew himself up. "I'm not afraid. Do it now. I would walk at your side in all things an equal. Even into battle. I would not have you fear for me."

"Lie back on the stones, then," I said.

Ilio reclined on the rocky bank. Despite his declaration, there was anxiety in his eyes as I leaned over him. "Open your mouth," I commanded, and when he obeyed, I brought up the black blood, the vile living fluid the Oombai called the *ebu potashu*. I put my mouth over his and the blood bolted out of my guts with a tearing pain. Ilio lurched, swallowing convulsively, his eyes wide. He kicked his legs and pushed against me, but his strength was no match for mine.

When I saw that it was adequate, and that he had

swallowed all of it, I released him.

He rolled away from me, shuddering and whining in pain. He curled into a tight ball, his face twisted. Every muscle in his body was spasming. It seemed his flesh blanched just a little bit whiter, became just a little bit harder; perhaps it was only my imagination. Eventually, the spasms passed and he uncurled his body. He rolled onto his back, gasping.

Seeing how little he had changed, I suggested we try again.

"No! No more!" he cried breathlessly. "The pain is too much! I can't bear it!"

"All right," I said quickly. "Not tonight."

"No," he said, crying a little and shaking his head. "No. Not tonight. Please."

"That's fine, Ilio. I promise, no more tonight. Can you rise?"

I could tell by his countenance that the pain was abating. He sat up and nodded his head. I took his hand and helped him to his feet.

"Let us feed," I said. "Tonight you will accompany me on a raid."

5

It was never my intention to allow him join my battle with the Elders, but I thought the boy would be safe enough if we should raid the warriors I'd seen camped upon the plains. I planned to avoid a direct confrontation with the men who were searching for us. I merely intended to pick a few stragglers from the edge of their encampment, steal some weapons and clothing and blood for our sustenance. Ilio, I felt sure, would be safe enough on this mission, and it would give him a bit of experience in such matters, experience he would require in the future, should we ever be parted.

At the rim of the great grassy plains, we climbed to the top of a tree and scanned the flatlands for their camp.

"There," I said, pointing.

As the moist wind whipped through our hair, we looked down upon the campfires glowing in the dark. The warriors had moved their camp closer. Much closer. "They saw your fire last night," I said to the boy, glancing toward him gravely.

Clinging to a swaying branch a few feet away, Ilio returned my grim stare. "They were coming for us?" he asked.

I nodded.

"I knew they were too far away to reach us before we rose," I said. "But we will have to abandon our muddy little hole and find someplace else to sleep come morning. Come, boy. We have much to do tonight." I released my grip and allowed my body to plummet to the ground. Bounding lightly from bough to bough, I landed in a crouch and awaited him.

Ilio dropped beside me. With the vampire child at my side, we moved swiftly through the grassland toward the warriors' camp.

As we travelled, I counseled him on our strategy, and upon the manner in which he must fortify his courage. To make war, I told him, one must put aside fear and sympathy. One must embrace the thought of death in battle as a glorious fate, and have no pity upon one's enemies, even if they cried and begged for mercy. To cling to either of those sentiments led only to failure. Both were a sure recipe for disaster.

"You must remove your mind away from your flesh when you make war," I said. "You must make of your body a weapon to be thrown upon your enemies. If your thoughts are free of fear and sympathy, your strategies will be more cunning, your success more assured."

"Your people must be great warriors," Ilio said admiringly.

I laughed. "No, we were very peaceful, but we knew that all living things must fight for their survival. It is an evident truth. You need only observe the world around you to see it. So we trained ourselves to fight, even as we enjoyed our days of plenty. We had no love for conflict, but we did not deny its necessity."

"It's easy to have no fear when you are strong," Ilio said, worrying perhaps about his small stature.

"The fight is won here," I said, pointing to my temple, and he nodded.

As we neared the encampment of the Oombai warriors, we slowed and took care where our feet fell. Staying low, we circled the camp stealthily. When we came upon a lone sentry, standing guard at a little distance from his fellow warriors, I put my hand on Ilio's shoulder to halt him and pointed toward the man, whose back was to us.

"See how that one longs for death?" I asked. "He stands at a distance from his brothers, with his back turned toward the night."

"He's watching the fire," Ilio whispered.

"I want you to take him. Move as quickly as you can. Cover his mouth with your hand and pull him into the darkness. Do not allow him to struggle or cry out. Bite his throat here on the side and drain his blood with all your might. Do it quickly, without pity, or return to our muddy hole now and await my return."

Ilio's eyes gleamed with hunger. I'd barely finished speaking when he shot from my side. Had I thought he needed encouragement? I'd underestimated his blood-thirst. I watched as he swept through the grass toward his target. If his back had not been turned toward us, the human might have seen a pale blur, if anything at all, though I could follow the boy's movements easily enough. He was fast. I watched him flash through the dark with new respect.

Ilio leaped like a crazed badger upon the larger man, knocking the sentry to the ground. Although their struggle was not as silent as I would have wished, the low grunts and cries were not loud enough to rouse any of the other warriors.

Ilio dragged the man away from the light of the campfires, his arms wrapped about the sentry's neck and shoulders. He jerked and wrenched his victim's body as he stumbled away with his prey, having a little bit of difficulty with the task, but only because he was inexperienced, not because he lacked strength. I moved to join him, and arrived in time to see Ilio duck his razor-sharp fangs to the doomed man's neck.

His victim bucked and kicked his legs as the boy drained him, but fell limp quickly enough. Ilio drained the man as I'd instructed. The warrior's body sagged. His arms rolled into the grass, fingers twitching.

Ilio's head jerked up as I drew near. His mouth and chin glittered with blood, black in the moonlight. His eyes were as feral as any wild predator guarding its prey from another.

He grinned then, the wild look in his eyes fading as he came back to himself. "It tastes good!" he sighed.

Then he dipped his mouth back to the man's neck.

Watching the boy make his first human kill filled me with horror and self-loathing. He was blameless in this crime, as he would be blameless in all the rest that were sure to follow. Out of weakness, out of loneliness, out of love, I had made him what he was-- a killer—in full knowledge of what that entailed... and in so doing, had unleashed more death on the world. His sins would forever belong to me. I would wear them like a stone about the neck.

The Oombai warrior's spirit had departed. I didn't want to look at the man's face, but my eyes were drawn to it nonetheless. Mouth drawn in pain, empty gaze rolled toward the moon, Ilio's victim silently accused. I ripped my gaze away, shame stabbing me deep in the guts.

"Come, boy," I whispered hoarsely. "Strip his body and take his weapons. We must hurry."

We hunted a while longer, claiming four victims-- two each-- before quitting the camp. Before we were finished, we were respectably clothed and armed. I'd even claimed a magnificent cape, one of dyed woven cloth trimmed in black crow's feathers. The mantle of a commander, who I killed as he shit in the weeds. We stole away into the night, our predations undiscovered and our bellies bulging with the hot blood of our enemies.

We traveled north until I felt we were a safe distance from the warriors who pursued us. In a thicket of pine, I embraced the boy and gave him some final instructions before I departed, just in case I didn't return.

Continue south, I told him. Look to your safety before all things, and refrain as much as possible from feeding on humans.

"You'll come back," he said, smiling at me confidently.

I returned his smile, then turned and blurred into flight.

6

In truth, I had every confidence I would return. I prepared the boy for the worst only because I knew: the outcome of battle is never a sure thing.

Fate is a fickle mistress. She had conspired to make me immortal. She had preserved me for untold millennia, even in the belly of a glacier. Yet, who could say when she would tire of my foolish endeavors? As I raced across the Pannonian Plain, all but flying beneath the lowering sky, I wondered if this night, by some disastrous misfortune, might be my last on earth.

And for what? I wondered.

Was this justice? Or petty revenge?

I like to think I am a peaceful man, that my heart is inured to such base emotion, but for all my vaunted powers, for all the eons I've walked this world, I am still a man. My soul is still a man's soul.

And those old men had offended me.

As I drew near the country of the Ground Scratchers, I prepared my heart for war. I gripped my purloined spear, set my mind apart so that it would not worry needlessly for the flesh that was its seat.

Light splashed the lowering heavens. Thunder rattled across the plains. Spicules of cold rain spattered my flesh as I hurtled through the night, each striking me painfully due to the speed at which I was racing.

Up ahead, flickering torches.

They were waiting for me.

Two lines of warriors stood, ready for battle, arranged in a narrowing corridor. There were some six or seven dozen warriors lined up, assembled on the plain at the edge of their village, eager to defend their masters. At the center of the phalanx, the three remaining elders waited, armed and armored. Hault stood in the middle of the trio, tall and imperious, a spear clutched in his hands. His weapon was large and ornately decorated, with a carved shaft and a large, curved stone point, more a symbol of office than an instrument of battle, but deadly all the same. On both sides of him crouched his cohorts Gant and Ungst, their bodies laden with fine armor made of bone and leather and lined with glossy black feathers. A great cry went up when their warriors caught sight of me.

I came to a stop, facing them across the whipping field of grass.

This place, this great open plain, would be the sight of countless battles through the ages. How many empires had skirmished here for supremacy? The Huns, the Gepids, the Ostrogoths. The Habsburgs and the Ottomans, too. But this night... this night was mine, a rogue vampire, intent on justice.

Rod Redux

"Depart from this country, Blood Drinker!" Hault demanded. He had to project his voice, as I'd paused a good distance away, cautious of his bowmen. "Go, and return here no more!"

I cannot give you an exact translation of what he said, as I was only halfway familiar with their tongue by then, but I am sure that was the gist of it.

"You have offended me, and I will have my vengeance!" I cried back at him. I spoke in the Denghoi tongue. Perhaps he understood me. Perhaps he only understood a little. Nevertheless, he shouted his rejoinder.

"I warn you. We have battled your kind before… and we have always triumphed!"

"Not tonight!" I roared, and then I bolted toward them.

Three dozen arrows whistled in my direction. In the dark, with the torch flames twisting and lightning pulsing in the heavens, it was difficult to mark each projectile that flitted toward me. I tried to dodge the weapons as they converged on me, pivoting this way and that, my hands snapping one direction and then another to slap them out of the air, but there were so many! Despite my superhuman speed and agility, I was impaled half a dozen times.

I stumbled to my knees, the shafts quivering in my flesh. There was one in my neck, three in my torso, and yet two more in my thigh and upper arm. I tore them from my flesh and rose to my feet. I could feel the Living Blood inside me, healing the wounds even as I stood. Before the bowmen could fire again, I cocked back my javelin and let it fly.

My spear flew straight and true. The elder Gant was bowled clear off his feet. In fact, I struck him down with such force that his feet came straight out of his boots. He rose, tottered forward with the shaft protruding from both sides of his torso, then he squawked once, clutching the shaft protruding from his heart, and collapsed.

Another barrage of arrows shurred in my direction.

Rather than try to dodge them on the ground, I leapt straight up. Lightning flared as I sliced through the heavens, great tongues of electricity racing across the contours of the lowering clouds. Time seemed to stretch in that stark white light, every drop of rain gleaming like a tiny jewel, every arrow hanging suspended as if from invisible threads-- even I, perched upon the wind, my stolen clothes and great black cloak flapping languidly, as if drifting underwater.

Then the night returned. I dropped to the ground.

Crouched in the center of the gauntlet, I bared my fangs and hissed. Several spears whisked toward me, and I plucked them from the air.

Leaping between the two remaining elders, I drove the spears into the fat one named Ungst, piercing him through. The plump old man bellowed in fury, blood bursting from his lips. I used the spears to drive him to his knees, then pushed him onto his back and pinned him to the loess. The whoremaster died, blood boiling out of his mouth in a bubbly red froth.

The smell of his blood enflamed my passion. I felt drunk with hunger and the sheer monstrous pleasure of murder, all the world painted red and slick and salty. I turned at last to Hault, my lips peeled back from my fangs, but before I could wrap my hands around his wattled neck, a strange weapon seized me by the shoulder.

It was an anchor with multiple hooks. Made of bone and attached to a long and slender woven cord, the strange weapon sunk its barb into my shoulder before I could puzzle out what I'd been snared by. An instant later, the rope went taut, and I stumbled back.

Another rope with a hooked anchor arced through the sky above me, and being reeled quickly in by the warrior who'd cast it, sank its flukes into my upper thigh.

Rod Redux

And another was cast upon me, and another. I felt myself hauled from the earth, my flesh ripping as the ropes were pulled ever tighter. If I were a lesser vampire, those barbed weapons would have been my doom. Even strong as I was, the clever ploy nearly bested me.

But I am powerful. If it were not so, how could I have endured some 30,000 years? For naught am I the oldest living vampire? No, this outlandish tactic would not defeat me!

Hault stalked toward me, thinking me beaten. The old man thrust his lance into my belly, his lips peeled back from yellow, crooked teeth. "DIE!" he shrieked in triumph.

Enraged, I grasped hold of the ropes suspending me from the ground and yanked them with all my strength. Some of the old man's warriors let go, the flesh stripped from their palms. Others were flung into the sky, their bodies pinwheeling away in the dark like windblown leaves. I dropped to the ground and lunged at Elder Hault.

His eyes went wide in shock and terror.

I grabbed him by the shoulders, and, with one swift jerk of my head, tore his throat out with my teeth.

7

My vengeance was fulfilled. Aioa's spirit could rest in the ghost world; Ilio's corruption was revenged.

The last of the Elders fell to his knees, his palms wrapped round the spurting hole in his windpipe. He gazed up at me, his gleaming eyes wide, filled with horrified disbelief. To make sure he was not preserved by the vampire blood he and his cohorts had used to prolong their lives, I cocked back my arm and struck his head from his shoulders. It went rolling away in the grass, and his body, taut and twitching, toppled onto its back.

But the spears and arrows continued to rain down around

me. I was struck in the back, the legs, the buttocks. Stubbornly ignoring the pain, I stalked to the body of Ungst and pulped his head with one stomp of my foot. I did the same to Elder Gant, and then I turned to face the horde of warriors encircling me.

They fell upon me, roaring, enraged. I threw myself into the mass of human bodies, howling like a demon. My assault was merciless. With my vampire strength, I tore their arms from their sockets, ripped their heads from their necks. I threw them into the air with all my strength. I was stabbed and slashed and bludgeoned, but each time I was knocked to my knees, I rose to battle on.

At last I fought my way free of the Oombai army and I leapt into the sky. As the heavens gave birth and the rain slashed down on the killing field in earnest, I withdrew.

I jumped clear of the battleground, but landed badly and sprawled onto my hands and knees. I paused for a moment to twist the spears and arrows from my cold white flesh, then gathered my strength and leapt again.

Wounded, exhausted, I returned to my son.

A New Path

1

It was dawn when I returned to the boy, but the morning light was tempered by the churning heavens, the clouds thick and gray. A cold rain lashed the plains, sweeping in twisting cold sheets across me. Ilio leapt to his feet when he saw me stumbling through the drumming deluge, my back bent, my body shot through with arrows and the broken shafts of several spears. I could not reach them all myself. He flew to me with a look of horror on his face and helped me to the thicket of evergreen trees where I'd instructed him to await me.

Sitting on a soft mound of pine needles, I allowed the boy to tend to my wounds. He pulled the spears and arrows from my flesh with a grim look on his face. Most of the wounds were deep enough to kill a mortal man.

I was no mortal, but their removal was painful nonetheless. Some of them he had to wriggle to and fro, and one was set so deep he could do naught but push it through to the other side of me and drag it out by the head.

"Is it done?" he asked. "Are you satisfied?" Tears rimmed his eyes as he asked me this—vampire tears, black and gummy.

"Yes," I said tiredly. "It is done."

He'd stripped off my wet cloak and outer coat, and watched as the living blood welled up in my wounds, slowly erasing them. Before he sat beside me, my flesh was white and flawless.

Once again, I am a gore-streaked spectacle, I thought to myself. My stolen clothes were tattered and soaked in human blood. My hands were gloved in bits of flesh and bone. My hair was dripping from the downpour, and the water that ran down my face was stained bright pink by all the human debris.

I stared south, toward the land of the Ground Scratchers, feeling little in my heart... only the physical sensations: cold, wet, exhausted.

"You need rest," the boy said finally. "Come. I made a shelter while you were gone."

He pulled me to my feet. I allowed him to escort me to the lean-to he'd constructed in my absence. It was quite large and comfortable, the floor padded with pine needles. I longed for a fire, a big, warm, crackling fire, but even for a vampire, that would have been a miraculous accomplishment in this torrential downpour.

Ilio spread out my cloak and I hunkered down and crawled inside. The boy joined me a moment later and covered the entrance with branches, blocking out the moist gray light.

"Where do we go now?" he asked in the dark.

"I don't know," I answered.

He put his head on my shoulder and I embraced him-- my boy, my son, my vampire child. "It doesn't matter," he said with a sigh. "You live. That's enough."

Listening to the thunder and the rhythmic susurration of the rain, I fell asleep.

2

I woke at twilight to the sound and smell of a terrified human being. Rising from my bedding, I pushed aside the branches covering the opening of Ilio's lean-to and stepped out into the thicket. The rain had moved on and the crickets in the woodland were buzzing merrily. I was still wet and there was no fire to warm my flesh and dry my clothing, but I paid little attention to my discomfort. My attention was riveted instead by the sight that greeted me upon rising.

Ilio had ventured out while I slept and returned now with a human captive. It was one of the Oombai warriors who had pursued us across the plains. Ilio dragged the man—who was at least two heads taller than the boy-- behind him by the ankles. The warrior was bound with leather cords, and lashed and twisted his body as the boy dragged him across the ground.

I walked out into the grass to meet them, the hunger inside me leaping at the sight of the trussed human.

"You need to eat," Ilio said, then dropped the man's legs. I could tell by the pink warmth of the boy's flesh that he had already fed.

The human was bruised and bleeding. When my gleaming eyes turned to him, the warrior began to yammer hysterically in his native tongue, his eyes wide with terror. I understood Oombai well enough by now, but I ignored his cries for mercy.

I lowered myself to my knees beside the flopping warrior. Pulling the man into my lap a little, I pushed his chin to the side and lowered my mouth to his plump, blood-filled flesh. As the warrior began to sob, despairing of his life, I sank my fangs into his neck. He stiffened and bucked, but I held him firmly and drained him as quickly as possible. I did not wish to make him suffer. I'd caused enough suffering of late.

When the man was dead and my appetite was sated, I rolled his carcass away and rose.

Ilio watched me with a faint smile, hoping perhaps for

some word of praise.

"You took care?" I asked.

He nodded. "This one was walking alone across the grassland. He didn't see me. I struck him down from behind and bound him with his own laces."

I could feel the warrior's blood inside me, the heat threading itself through my veins. The last few aches and pains from the previous night's battle throbbed and faded. I smiled at the boy, touched by his care. His love—perhaps even more than the blood—strengthened me.

"Where do we go now?" I asked.

"When I was hunting, I saw a group of humans traveling east," Ilio replied. "I think it was some of the slaves the Oombai kept. The Neirie. There was a column of smoke rising from the village of the Ground Scratchers, too. Perhaps the slaves rose up and won their freedom."

"Should we follow them?"

Ilio shrugged. "Maybe we should seek the other Blood Drinkers, the ones the Elders spoke of. I would like to know what they are like."

We returned to the lean-to and I fetched my cloak. It was still wet and stank of blood, but I was reluctant to discard such a fine piece of clothing. I threw it over my shoulders and tied the laces, grimacing a little at the smell... and at my own ripe stench. I would have to bathe and wash my soiled garments before the odor drove me to distraction.

"And what if these Blood Drinkers are the ones who attacked your village, Ilio?" I questioned him. "What if they're the ones who massacred the Denghoi?"

Ilio sighed. "I don't know. I know now the hunger that presses our kind to violence. Perhaps... if they are kind like you... and not cruel and wanton... I can forgive them their trespasses." He looked up at me as we started across the grassland. "It would be nice to live among our own kind, don't you think?"

Thinking of the destroyed Denghoi camp, I was not overly enamored with the thought… or the prospect of their kindness. I remembered my terrible excitement when I first caught their spore, but now…

"Perhaps," I said. "Let us follow the humans for a little while, first. But we must be careful to stay at a safe distance from them, so that we are not tempted to harm them. It would not do to free them from one set of masters, only to give in to our own base desires."

I surveyed the plains as we walked, the rolling hills, retreating in all directions.

"These lands are still unfamiliar to me. We may come across those other Blood Drinkers by chance, or choose to seek them out later, but for now, let us watch over and protect the humans who escaped those greedy Oombai. We can be their guardian spirits for a little while. Is that agreeable to your thinking?"

Ilio considered the idea. His smile flashed out at me, white and pointed. "Yes, that would be a good thing!" he said.

Liege, Belgium
6:30 am, December 23, 2010 A.D.

"And so that's it?" the German demanded.

"Hardly," I replied. "But I'm afraid that's all the time we have tonight." I nodded toward the brightening balcony doors, the low December light pressing to the frosted glass.

I'd bound him to another chair after knocking him unconscious, and he glowered at me, his face bruised and swollen. "You've told me nothing. Just a story about how you killed some corrupt old men."

I shrugged. "It is what it is. Life is not plotted like a novel."

The German snorted with derision. "I thought you would tell me something important. Some grand revelation."

"Such as…?"

"I don't know," my captive said sullenly. "Does it matter if we're good or bad? Is there life after death? Is there a God?"

I chuckled. "For our sake, I hope not."

Suddenly furious, the pornographer lashed in his bonds. Spittle flew from his lips as he screamed at me: "I listened to you all night long! What was the point? You're the oldest living thing in the world, and you're no wiser than anyone else!"

"I told you," I replied calmly. "This grand revelation you were hoping for. I did tell you. You just didn't grasp it."

He stopped struggling. Nostrils flaring, he glared at me. "What? If there is some meaning in your tale, then explain it to me, or finish me now. I'm tired of waiting for you to kill me. My body aches, and I have to shit. I'm tired of being tied to this chair, for fuck's sake. Tell me!"

"I have lived for thirty thousand years," I whispered, leaning toward him dramatically. "For all my time in this world, for all my experiences, I've discovered only one thing ever really matters."

"What is it? Tell me!"

I leapt on him then. With a snarl, I seized him and brought my fangs to his neck. He screamed in anguish as I bit into his flesh, severing his carotid and jugular with one quick slash. The blood gushed out of him, hot and salty, filling my mouth, spilling down my chin. I grabbed his hair and jerked his head to the side and sucked his life out in great, greedy draughts. I filled my belly with him, and when he was a hair's breadth from death, I brought the Living Blood up from the center of me, and I spat it onto the spraying wound.

I stepped back and watched the black blood knit the ragged tears back together. The bleeding slowed... stopped. His eyes rolled groggily toward me. He was pale with blood loss, only half-conscious.

"Why?" he croaked.

"Because I can. Because you deserve this," I said. I smiled. "I have many more tales to tell you."

Adieu, For Now

Evening comes as I complete this second volume of my memoirs. In just a few hours, it will be Christmas morning, a celebration of the birth of a radical young rabbi named Yeshua, who was delivered—or so the story goes—in the manger of a donkey, some two thousand years ago.

Was he really the son of God?

I don't know.

I've seen a lot of messiahs come and go in thirty thousand years. But I've always liked the message he preached. It's too bad no one really understands it. Instead, the powerful use his name to draw lines on the battlefield of our souls. The weak retreat into its shadow.

I think he would weep if he knew the atrocities that have been committed in his name. I'm sure of it, actually. I wish I had met him, but I was living in Rome when he ministered to the Jews.

In the adjacent room, my captive audience sleeps fitfully in his chair. I can hear his soft snores. I can smell the rank odor of his excrement. He soiled himself sometime during the day, while I slept in the guest room on the other side of the suite.

I'm not sure why I've let him live, only that I'm not finished with him. I want to tell him more, and I want him to tell me more as well.

But for now this tale is told. Perhaps it's too brief. I'm ever

Rod Redux

insecure of my literary talents, but I didn't want to encumber you with some thick and clumsy tome. I'm afraid I may grow tiresome if I ramble on too long.

I hope you are still curious about me. I hope you'll read the volumes to follow. I promise there is a meaning to it all. No Grand Revelation, perhaps, but a truth, a real truth, and a good one.

I'm sure, if you're a wise and virtuous person, you've already figured out what it is. I'm loath to write it out explicitly, only because it sounds cliché, and maybe you won't read any more of my stories if I do.

For now, I bid you adieu.

Until we meet again, I remain your friend,

Gon,
The Oldest Living Vampire

About the Author

Rod Redux lives in Southern Illinois with his wife, his kids and all the voices in his head. This is his fourth novel.

The Oldest Living Vampire
The Prehistoric Cycle

Book One
The Oldest Living Vampire Tells All

Book Two
The Oldest Living Vampire on the Prowl

Book Three
The Oldest Living Vampire in Love
(December 2011)

Book Four
The Oldest Living Vampire Reborn
(2012)

Book Five
The Oldest Living Vampire Unleashed
(2012)

Made in the USA
Lexington, KY
12 January 2012